D0535729

Charlotte's Web

E. B. White
Pictures by Garth Williams

HARPER
An Imprint of HarperCollinsPublishers

HarperCollins
PUBLISHERS
Since 1817

Charlotte's Web
Copyright 1952 by E. B. White
Text copyright © renewed 1980 by E. B. White
Illustrations copyright © renewed 1980 by Estate of Garth Williams

For information address HarperCollins Children's Books, a division
of HarperCollins Publishers, 195 Broadway,
New York, NY 10007.
www.harpercollinschildrens.com
ISBN 978-0-06-265875-3

17 18 19 20 21   PC/LSCH   10 9 8 7 6 5 4 3 2 1
Harper Classic edition, 2017

Contents

I. Before Breakfast

"WHERE'S Papa going with that ax?" said Fern to her mother as they were setting the table for breakfast.

"Out to the hoghouse," replied Mrs. Arable. "Some pigs were born last night."

"I don't see why he needs an ax," continued Fern, who was only eight.

"Well," said her mother, "one of the pigs is a runt. It's very small and weak, and it will never amount to anything. So your father has decided to do away with it."

"Do *away* with it?" shrieked Fern. "You mean *kill* it? Just because it's smaller than the others?"

Mrs. Arable put a pitcher of cream on the table. "Don't yell, Fern!" she said. "Your father is right. The pig would probably die anyway."

Fern pushed a chair out of the way and ran outdoors. The grass was wet and the earth smelled of springtime. Fern's sneakers were sopping by the time she caught up with her father.

"Please don't kill it!" she sobbed. "It's unfair."

Mr. Arable stopped walking.

"Fern," he said gently, "you will have to learn to control yourself."

"Control myself?" yelled Fern. "This is a matter of life and death, and you talk about *controlling* myself."

Tears ran down her cheeks and she took hold of the ax and tried to pull it out of her father's hand.

"Fern," said Mr. Arable, "I know more about raising a litter of pigs than you do. A weakling makes trouble. Now run along!"

"But it's unfair," cried Fern. "The pig couldn't help being born small, could it? If *I* had been very small at birth, would you have killed *me*?"

Mr. Arable smiled. "Certainly not," he said, looking down at his daughter with love. "But this is different. A little girl is one thing, a little runty pig is another."

"I see no difference," replied Fern, still hanging on to the ax. "This is the most terrible case of injustice I ever heard of."

A queer look came over John Arable's face. He seemed almost ready to cry himself.

"All right," he said. "You go back to the house and I will bring the runt when I come in. I'll let you start it on a bottle, like a baby. Then you'll see what trouble a pig can be."

When Mr. Arable returned to the house half an hour later, he carried a carton under his arm. Fern was upstairs changing her sneakers. The kitchen table was set for breakfast, and the room smelled of coffee, bacon, damp plaster, and wood smoke from the stove.

"Put it on her chair!" said Mrs. Arable. Mr. Arable set the carton down at Fern's place. Then he walked to the sink and washed his hands and dried them on the roller towel.

Fern came slowly down the stairs. Her eyes were red from crying. As she approached her chair, the carton wobbled, and there was a scratching noise. Fern looked at her father. Then she lifted the lid of the carton. There, inside, looking up at her, was the newborn pig. It was a white one. The morning light shone through its ears, turning them pink.

"He's yours," said Mr. Arable. "Saved from an untimely death. And may the good Lord forgive me for this foolishness."

Fern couldn't take her eyes off the tiny pig. "Oh," she whispered. "Oh, *look* at him! He's absolutely perfect."

She closed the carton carefully. First she kissed her father, then she kissed her mother. Then she opened the lid again, lifted the pig out, and held it against her cheek. At this moment her brother Avery came into the room. Avery was ten. He was heavily armed —an air rifle in one hand, a wooden dagger in the other.

"What's that?" he demanded. "What's Fern got?"

"She's got a guest for breakfast," said Mrs. Arable. "Wash your hands and face, Avery!"

"Let's see it!" said Avery, setting his gun down. "You call that miserable thing a pig? That's a *fine* specimen of a pig—it's no bigger than a white rat."

"Wash up and eat your breakfast, Avery!" said his mother. "The school bus will be along in half an hour."

"Can I have a pig, too, Pop?" asked Avery.

"No, I only distribute pigs to early risers," said Mr. Arable. "Fern was up at daylight, trying to rid the world of injustice. As a result, she now has a pig. A small one, to be sure, but nevertheless a pig. It just shows what can happen if a person gets out of bed promptly. Let's eat!"

But Fern couldn't eat until her pig had had a drink of milk. Mrs. Arable found a baby's nursing bottle and a rubber nipple. She poured warm milk into the bottle, fitted the nipple over the top, and handed it to Fern. "Give him his breakfast!" she said.

A minute later, Fern was seated on the floor in the corner of the kitchen with her infant between her knees, teaching it to suck from the bottle. The pig, although tiny, had a good appetite and caught on quickly.

The school bus honked from the road.

"Run!" commanded Mrs. Arable, taking the pig from Fern and slipping a doughnut into her hand. Avery grabbed his gun and another doughnut.

The children ran out to the road and climbed into the bus. Fern took no notice of the others in the bus. She just sat and stared out of the window, thinking what a blissful world it was and how lucky she was to have entire charge of a pig. By the time the bus reached school, Fern had named her pet, selecting the most beautiful name she could think of.

"Its name is Wilbur," she whispered to herself.

She was still thinking about the pig when the teacher said: "Fern, what is the capital of Pennsylvania?"

"Wilbur," replied Fern, dreamily. The pupils giggled. Fern blushed.

II. Wilbur

FERN loved Wilbur more than anything. She loved to stroke him, to feed him, to put him to bed. Every morning, as soon as she got up, she warmed his milk, tied his bib on, and held the bottle for him. Every afternoon, when the school bus stopped in front of her house, she jumped out and ran to the kitchen to fix another bottle for him. She fed him again at suppertime, and again just before going to bed. Mrs. Arable gave him a feeding around noontime each day, when Fern was away in school. Wilbur loved his milk, and he was never happier than when Fern was warming up a bottle for him. He would stand and gaze up at her with adoring eyes.

For the first few days of his life, Wilbur was allowed to live in a box near the stove in the kitchen. Then, when Mrs. Arable complained, he was moved to a bigger box in the woodshed. At two weeks of age, he was moved outdoors. It was apple-blossom time, and the days were getting warmer. Mr. Arable fixed a small yard specially for Wilbur under an apple tree, and

gave him a large wooden box full of straw, with a
doorway cut in it so he could walk in and out as he
pleased.

"Won't he be cold at night?" asked Fern.

"No," said her father. "You watch and see what he
does."

Carrying a bottle of milk, Fern sat down under the

apple tree inside the yard. Wilbur ran to her and she
held the bottle for him while he sucked. When he had
finished the last drop, he grunted and walked sleepily
into the box. Fern peered through the door. Wilbur
was poking the straw with his snout. In a short time
he had dug a tunnel in the straw. He crawled into the
tunnel and disappeared from sight, completely covered with straw. Fern was enchanted. It relieved her
mind to know that her baby would sleep covered up,
and would stay warm.

Every morning after breakfast, Wilbur walked out to the road with Fern and waited with her till the bus came. She would wave good-bye to him, and he would stand and watch the bus until it vanished around a turn. While Fern was in school, Wilbur was shut up inside his yard. But as soon as she got home in the afternoon, she would take him out and he would follow her around the place. If she went into the house, Wilbur went, too. If she went upstairs, Wilbur would wait at the bottom step until she came down again. If she took her doll for a walk in the doll carriage, Wilbur followed along. Sometimes, on these journeys, Wilbur would get tired, and Fern would pick him up and put him in the carriage alongside the doll. He liked this. And if he was *very* tired, he would close his eyes and go to sleep under the doll's blanket. He looked cute when his eyes were closed, because his lashes were so long. The doll would close her eyes, too, and Fern would wheel the carriage very slowly and smoothly so as not to wake her infants.

One warm afternoon, Fern and Avery put on bathing suits and went down to the brook for a swim. Wilbur tagged along at Fern's heels. When she waded into the brook, Wilbur waded in with her. He found the water quite cold—too cold for his liking. So while the children swam and played and splashed water at each other, Wilbur amused himself in the mud along the edge of the brook, where it was warm and moist and delightfully sticky and oozy.

Every day was a happy day, and every night was peaceful.

Wilbur was what farmers call a spring pig, which simply means that he was born in springtime. When he was five weeks old, Mr. Arable said he was now big enough to sell, and would have to be sold. Fern broke down and wept. But her father was firm about it. Wilbur's appetite had increased; he was beginning to eat scraps of food in addition to milk. Mr. Arable was not willing to provide for him any longer. He had already sold Wilbur's ten brothers and sisters.

"He's got to go, Fern," he said. "You have had your fun raising a baby pig, but Wilbur is not a baby any longer and he has got to be sold."

"Call up the Zuckermans," suggested Mrs. Arable to Fern. "Your Uncle Homer sometimes raises a pig. And if Wilbur goes there to live, you can walk down the road and visit him as often as you like."

"How much money should I ask for him?" Fern wanted to know.

"Well," said her father, "he's a runt. Tell your Uncle Homer you've got a pig you'll sell for six dollars, and see what he says."

It was soon arranged. Fern phoned and got her Aunt Edith, and her Aunt Edith hollered for Uncle Homer, and Uncle Homer came in from the barn and talked to Fern. When he heard that the price was only six dollars, he said he would buy the pig. Next day Wilbur was taken from his home under the apple tree and went to live in a manure pile in the cellar of Zuckerman's barn.

III. *Escape*

THE BARN was very large. It was very old. It smelled of hay and it smelled of manure. It smelled of the perspiration of tired horses and the wonderful sweet breath of patient cows. It often had a sort of peaceful smell—as though nothing bad could happen ever again in the world. It smelled of grain and of harness dressing and of axle grease and of rubber boots and of new rope. And whenever the cat was given a fish-head to eat, the barn would smell of fish. But mostly it smelled of hay, for there was always hay in the great loft up overhead. And there was always hay being pitched down to the cows and the horses and the sheep.

The barn was pleasantly warm in winter when the animals spent most of their time indoors, and it was pleasantly cool in summer when the big doors stood wide open to the breeze. The barn had stalls on the main floor for the work horses, tie-ups on the main floor for the cows, a sheepfold down below for the sheep, a pigpen down below for Wilbur, and it was

full of all sorts of things that you find in barns: ladders,
grindstones, pitch forks, monkey wrenches, scythes,
lawn mowers, snow shovels, ax handles, milk pails,
water buckets, empty grain sacks, and rusty rat traps.
It was the kind of barn that swallows like to build their
nests in. It was the kind of barn that children like to
play in. And the whole thing was owned by Fern's
uncle, Mr. Homer L. Zuckerman.

Wilbur's new home was in the lower part of the
barn, directly underneath the cows. Mr. Zuckerman
knew that a manure pile is a good place to keep a young
pig. Pigs need warmth, and it was warm and comfortable down there in the barn cellar on the south
side.

Fern came almost every day to visit him. She found

an old milking stool that had been discarded, and she placed the stool in the sheepfold next to Wilbur's pen. Here she sat quietly during the long afternoons, thinking and listening and watching Wilbur. The

sheep soon got to know her and trust her. So did the geese, who lived with the sheep. All the animals trusted her, she was so quiet and friendly. Mr. Zuckerman did not allow her to take Wilbur out, and he did not allow her to get into the pigpen. But he told Fern that she could sit on the stool and watch Wilbur as long as she wanted to. It made her happy just to be near the pig, and it made Wilbur happy to know that she was sitting there, right outside his pen. But he never had any fun— no walks, no rides, no swims.

One afternoon in June, when Wilbur was almost two months old, he wandered out into his small yard outside the barn. Fern had not arrived for her usual visit. Wilbur stood in the sun feeling lonely and bored.

"There's never anything to do around here," he thought. He walked slowly to his food trough and sniffed to see if anything had been overlooked at lunch. He found a small strip of potato skin and ate it. His back itched, so he leaned against the fence and rubbed against the boards. When he tired of this, he walked indoors, climbed to the top of the manure pile, and sat down. He didn't feel like going to sleep, he didn't feel like digging, he was tired of standing still, tired of lying down. "I'm less than two months old and I'm tired of living," he said. He walked out to the yard again.

"When I'm out here," he said, "there's no place to go but in. When I'm indoors, there's no place to go but out in the yard."

"That's where you're wrong, my friend, my friend," said a voice.

Wilbur looked through the fence and saw the goose standing there.

"You don't have to stay in that dirty-little dirty-little dirty-little yard," said the goose, who talked rather fast. "One of the boards is loose. Push on it, push-push-push on it, and come on out!"

"What?" said Wilbur. "Say it slower!"

"At-at-at, at the risk of repeating myself," said the goose, "I suggest that you come on out. It's wonderful out here."

"Did you say a board was loose?"

"That I did, that I did," said the goose.

Wilbur walked up to the fence and saw that the goose was right—one board was loose. He put his head down, shut his eyes, and pushed. The board gave way. In a minute he had squeezed through the fence and was standing in the long grass outside his yard. The goose chuckled.

"How does it feel to be free?" she asked.

"I like it," said Wilbur. "That is, I *guess* I like it." Actually, Wilbur felt queer to be outside his fence, with nothing between him and the big world.

"Where do you think I'd better go?"

"Anywhere you like, anywhere you like," said the goose. "Go down through the orchard, root up the sod! Go down through the garden, dig up the radishes! Root up everything! Eat grass! Look for corn! Look for oats! Run all over! Skip and dance, jump and prance! Go down through the orchard and stroll in the woods! The world is a wonderful place when you're young."

"I can see that," replied Wilbur. He gave a jump in the air, twirled, ran a few steps, stopped, looked all around, sniffed the smells of afternoon, and then set off walking down through the orchard. Pausing in the shade of an apple tree, he put his strong snout into the ground and began pushing, digging, and rooting. He felt very happy. He had plowed up quite a piece of ground before anyone noticed him. Mrs. Zuckerman was the first to see him. She saw him from the kitchen window, and she immediately shouted for the men.

"Ho-*mer*!" she cried. "Pig's out! Lurvy! Pig's out! Homer! Lurvy! Pig's out. He's down there under that apple tree."

"Now the trouble starts," thought Wilbur. "Now I'll catch it."

The goose heard the racket and she, too, started hollering. "Run-run-run downhill, make for the woods, the woods!" she shouted to Wilbur. "They'll never-never-never catch you in the woods."

The cocker spaniel heard the commotion and he ran out from the barn to join the chase. Mr. Zuckerman heard, and he came out of the machine shed where he was mending a tool. Lurvy, the hired man, heard the noise and came up from the asparagus patch where he was pulling weeds. Everybody walked toward Wilbur and Wilbur didn't know what to do. The woods seemed a long way off, and anyway, he had never been down there in the woods and wasn't sure he would like it.

"Get around behind him, Lurvy," said Mr. Zuckerman, "and drive him toward the barn! And take it easy—don't rush him! I'll go and get a bucket of slops."

The news of Wilbur's escape spread rapidly among the animals on the place. Whenever any creature broke loose on Zuckerman's farm, the event was of great interest to the others. The goose shouted to the nearest cow that Wilbur was free, and soon all the cows knew. Then one of the cows told one of the sheep, and soon all the sheep knew. The lambs learned about it from their mothers. The horses, in their stalls in the barn, pricked up their ears when they heard the goose hollering; and soon the horses had caught on to what was happening. "Wilbur's out," they said. Every animal stirred and lifted its head and became excited to know that one of his friends had got free and was no longer penned up or tied fast.

Wilbur didn't know what to do or which way to run. It seemed as though everybody was after him. "If this is what it's like to be free," he thought, "I believe I'd rather be penned up in my own yard."

The cocker spaniel was sneaking up on him from one

side, Lurvy the hired man was sneaking up on him from the other side. Mrs. Zuckerman stood ready to head him off if he started for the garden, and now Mr. Zuckerman was coming down toward him carrying a pail. "This is really awful," thought Wilbur. "Why doesn't Fern come?" He began to cry.

The goose took command and began to give orders.

"Don't just stand there, Wilbur! Dodge about, dodge about!" cried the goose. "Skip around, run toward me, slip in and out, in and out, in and out! Make for the woods! Twist and turn!"

The cocker spaniel sprang for Wilbur's hind leg. Wilbur jumped and ran. Lurvy reached out and grabbed. Mrs. Zuckerman screamed at Lurvy. The goose cheered for Wilbur. Wilbur dodged between

Lurvy's legs. Lurvy missed Wilbur and grabbed the spaniel instead. "Nicely done, nicely done!" cried the goose. "Try it again, try it again!"

"Run downhill!" suggested the cows.

"Run toward me!" yelled the gander.

"Run uphill!" cried the sheep.

"Turn and twist!" honked the goose.

"Jump and dance!" said the rooster.

"Look out for Lurvy!" called the cows.

"Look out for Zuckerman!" yelled the gander.

"Watch out for the dog!" cried the sheep.

"Listen to me, listen to me!" screamed the goose.

Poor Wilbur was dazed and frightened by this hulla-baloo. He didn't like being the center of all this fuss. He tried to follow the instructions his friends were giving him, but he couldn't run downhill and uphill at the same time, and he couldn't turn and twist when he was jumping and dancing, and he was crying so hard he could barely see anything that was happening. After all, Wilbur was a very young pig—not much more than a baby, really. He wished Fern were there to take him in her arms and comfort him. When he looked up and saw Mr. Zuckerman standing quite close to him, holding a pail of warm slops, he felt relieved. He lifted his nose and sniffed. The smell was delicious —warm milk, potato skins, wheat middlings, Kellogg's Corn Flakes, and a popover left from the Zuckermans' breakfast.

"Come, pig!" said Mr. Zuckerman, tapping the pail. "Come pig!"

Wilbur took a step toward the pail.

"No-no-no!" said the goose. "It's the old pail trick, Wilbur. Don't fall for it, don't fall for it! He's trying to lure you back into captivity-ivity. He's appealing to your stomach."

Wilbur didn't care. The food smelled appetizing. He took another step toward the pail.

"Pig, pig!" said Mr. Zuckerman in a kind voice, and began walking slowly toward the barnyard, looking all about him innocently, as if he didn't know that a little white pig was following along behind him.

"You'll be sorry-sorry-sorry," called the goose.

Wilbur didn't care. He kept walking toward the pail of slops.

"You'll miss your freedom," honked the goose. "An hour of freedom is worth a barrel of slops."

Wilbur didn't care.

When Mr. Zuckerman reached the pigpen, he climbed over the fence and poured the slops into the trough. Then he pulled the loose board away from the fence, so that there was a wide hole for Wilbur to walk through.

"Reconsider, reconsider!" cried the goose.

Wilbur paid no attention. He stepped through the fence into his yard. He walked to the trough and took a long drink of slops, sucking in the milk hungrily and chewing the popover. It was good to be home again.

While Wilbur ate, Lurvy fetched a hammer and some 8-penny nails and nailed the board in place. Then he and Mr. Zuckerman leaned lazily on the fence and Mr. Zuckerman scratched Wilbur's back with a stick.

"He's quite a pig," said Lurvy.

"Yes, he'll make a good pig," said Mr. Zuckerman. Wilbur heard the words of praise. He felt the warm milk inside his stomach. He felt the pleasant rubbing of the stick along his itchy back. He felt peaceful and happy and sleepy. This had been a tiring afternoon. It was still only about four o'clock but Wilbur was ready for bed.

"I'm really too young to go out into the world alone," he thought as he lay down.

IV. Loneliness

THE NEXT day was rainy and dark. Rain fell on the roof of the barn and dripped steadily from the eaves. Rain fell in the barnyard and ran in crooked courses down into the lane where thistles and pigweed grew. Rain spattered against Mrs. Zuckerman's kitchen windows and came gushing out of the downspouts. Rain fell on the backs of the sheep as they grazed in the meadow. When the sheep tired of standing in the rain, they walked slowly up the lane and into the fold.

Rain upset Wilbur's plans. Wilbur had planned to go out, this day, and dig a new hole in his yard. He had other plans, too. His plans for the day went something like this:

Breakfast at six-thirty. Skim milk, crusts, middlings, bits of doughnuts, wheat cakes with drops of maple syrup sticking to them, potato skins, leftover custard pudding with raisins, and bits of Shredded Wheat.

Breakfast would be finished at seven.

From seven to eight, Wilbur planned to have a talk

with Templeton, the rat that lived under his trough. Talking with Templeton was not the most interesting occupation in the world but it was better than nothing.

From eight to nine, Wilbur planned to take a nap outdoors in the sun.

From nine to eleven he planned to dig a hole, or trench, and possibly find something good to eat buried in the dirt.

From eleven to twelve he planned to stand still and watch flies on the boards, watch bees in the clover, and watch swallows in the air.

Twelve o'clock—lunchtime. Middlings, warm water, apple parings, meat gravy, carrot scrapings, meat scraps, stale hominy, and the wrapper off a package of cheese. Lunch would be over at one.

From one to two, Wilbur planned to sleep.

From two to three, he planned to scratch itchy places by rubbing against the fence.

From three to four, he planned to stand perfectly still and think of what it was like to be alive, and to wait for Fern.

At four would come supper. Skim milk, provender, leftover sandwich from Lurvy's lunchbox, prune skins, a morsel of this, a bit of that, fried potatoes, marmalade drippings, a little more of this, a little more of that, a piece of baked apple, a scrap of upsidedown cake.

Wilbur had gone to sleep thinking about these plans.

He awoke at six and saw the rain, and it seemed as though he couldn't bear it.

"I get everything all beautifully planned out and it has to go and rain," he said.

For a while he stood gloomily indoors. Then he walked to the door and looked out. Drops of rain struck his face. His yard was cold and wet. His trough had an inch of rainwater in it. Templeton was nowhere to be seen.

"Are you out there, Templeton?" called Wilbur. There was no answer. Suddenly Wilbur felt lonely and friendless.

"One day just like another," he groaned. "I'm very young, I have no real friend here in the barn, it's going to rain all morning and all afternoon, and Fern won't come in such bad weather. Oh, *honestly!*" And Wilbur was crying again, for the second time in two days.

At six-thirty Wilbur heard the banging of a pail. Lurvy was standing outside in the rain, stirring up breakfast.

"C'mon, pig!" said Lurvy.

Wilbur did not budge. Lurvy dumped the slops, scraped the pail, and walked away. He noticed that something was wrong with the pig.

Wilbur didn't want food, he wanted love. He wanted a friend—someone who would play with him. He mentioned this to the goose, who was sitting quietly in a corner of the sheepfold.

"Will you come over and play with me?" he asked.

"Sorry, sonny, sorry," said the goose. "I'm sitting-sitting on my eggs. Eight of them. Got to keep them toasty-oasty-oasty warm. I have to stay right here, I'm no flibberty-ibberty-gibbet. I do not play when there are eggs to hatch. I'm expecting goslings."

"Well, I didn't think you were expecting wood-peckers," said Wilbur, bitterly.

Wilbur next tried one of the lambs.

"Will you please play with me?" he asked.

"Certainly not," said the lamb. "In the first place, I cannot get into your pen, as I am not old enough to jump over the fence. In the second place, I am not in-terested in pigs. Pigs mean less than nothing to me."

"What do you mean, *less* than nothing?" replied Wilbur. "I don't think there is any such thing as *less* than nothing. Nothing is absolutely the limit of noth-ingness. It's the lowest you can go. It's the end of the line. How can something be less than nothing? If there were something that was less than nothing, then noth-ing would not be nothing, it would be something— even though it's just a very little bit of something. But if nothing is *nothing*, then nothing has nothing that is less than *it* is."

"Oh, be quiet!" said the lamb. "Go play by yourself! I don't play with pigs."

Sadly, Wilbur lay down and listened to the rain. Soon he saw the rat climbing down a slanting board that he used as a stairway.

"Will you play with me, Templeton?" asked Wilbur.

"Play?" said Templeton, twirling his whiskers. "Play? I hardly know the meaning of the word."

"Well," said Wilbur, "it means to have fun, to frolic, to run and skip and make merry."

"I never do those things if I can avoid them," replied the rat, sourly. "I prefer to spend my time eating, gnawing, spying, and hiding. I am a glutton but not a merrymaker. Right now I am on my way to your trough to eat your breakfast, since you haven't got sense enough to eat it yourself." And Templeton, the rat, crept stealthily along the wall and disappeared into a private tunnel that he had dug between the door and the trough in Wilbur's yard. Templeton was a crafty rat, and he had things pretty much his own way. The tunnel was an example of his skill and cunning. The tunnel enabled him to get from the barn to his hiding place under the pig trough without coming out into the open. He had tunnels and runways all over Mr. Zuckerman's farm and could get from one place to another without being seen. Usually he slept during the daytime and was abroad only after dark.

Wilbur watched him disappear into his tunnel. In a moment he saw the rat's sharp nose poke out from underneath the wooden trough. Cautiously Templeton pulled himself up over the edge of the trough. This was almost more than Wilbur could stand: on this dreary, rainy day to see his breakfast being eaten by somebody else. He knew Templeton was getting soaked, out there in the pouring rain, but even that didn't comfort him. Friendless, dejected, and hungry, he threw himself down in the manure and sobbed.

Late that afternoon, Lurvy went to Mr. Zuckerman. "I think there's something wrong with that pig of yours. He hasn't touched his food."

"Give him two spoonfuls of sulphur and a little mo-
lasses," said Mr. Zuckerman.

Wilbur couldn't believe what was happening to him
when Lurvy caught him and forced the medicine down
his throat. This was certainly the worst day of his life.
He didn't know whether he could endure the awful
loneliness any more.

Darkness settled over everything. Soon there were
only shadows and the noises of the sheep chewing their
cuds, and occasionally the rattle of a cow-chain up
overhead. You can imagine Wilbur's surprise when,
out of the darkness, came a small voice he had never
heard before. It sounded rather thin, but pleasant. "Do
you want a friend, Wilbur?" it said. "I'll be a friend to
you. I've watched you all day and I like you."

"But I can't see you," said Wilbur, jumping to his
feet. "Where are you? And *who* are you?"

"I'm right up here," said the voice. "Go to sleep.
You'll see me in the morning."

V. *Charlotte*

THE NIGHT seemed long. Wilbur's stomach was empty and his mind was full. And when your stomach is empty and your mind is full, it's always hard to sleep.

A dozen times during the night Wilbur woke and stared into the blackness, listening to the sounds and trying to figure out what time it was. A barn is never perfectly quiet. Even at midnight there is usually something stirring.

The first time he woke, he heard Templeton gnawing a hole in the grain bin. Templeton's teeth scraped loudly against the wood and made quite a racket. "That crazy rat!" thought Wilbur. "Why does he have to stay up all night, grinding his clashers and destroying people's property? Why can't he go to sleep, like any decent animal?"

The second time Wilbur woke, he heard the goose turning on her nest and chuckling to herself.

"What time is it?" whispered Wilbur to the goose.

"Probably-obably-obably about half-past eleven," said the goose. "Why aren't you asleep, Wilbur?"

"Too many things on my mind," said Wilbur.

"Well," said the goose, "that's not *my* trouble. I have nothing at all on my mind, but I've too many things under my behind. Have you ever tried to sleep while sitting on eight eggs?"

"No," replied Wilbur. "I suppose it *is* uncomfortable. How long does it take a goose egg to hatch?"

"Approximately-oximately thirty days, all told," answered the goose. "But I cheat a little. On warm afternoons, I just pull a little straw over the eggs and go out for a walk."

Wilbur yawned and went back to sleep. In his dreams he heard again the voice saying, "I'll be a friend to you. Go to sleep—you'll see me in the morning."

About half an hour before dawn, Wilbur woke and listened. The barn was still dark. The sheep lay motionless. Even the goose was quiet. Overhead, on the main floor, nothing stirred: the cows were resting, the horses dozed. Templeton had quit work and gone off somewhere on an errand. The only sound was a slight scraping noise from the rooftop, where the weather-vane swung back and forth. Wilbur loved the barn when it was like this—calm and quiet, waiting for light.

"Day is almost here," he thought.

Through a small window, a faint gleam appeared.

One by one the stars went out. Wilbur could see the goose a few feet away. She sat with head tucked under a wing. Then he could see the sheep and the lambs. The sky lightened.

"Oh, beautiful day, it is here at last! Today I shall find my friend."

Wilbur looked everywhere. He searched his pen thoroughly. He examined the window ledge, stared up at the ceiling. But he saw nothing new. Finally he decided he would have to speak up. He hated to break the lovely stillness of dawn by using his voice, but he couldn't think of any other way to locate the mysterious new friend who was nowhere to be seen. So Wilbur cleared his throat.

"Attention, please!" he said in a loud, firm voice. "Will the party who addressed me at bedtime last night kindly make himself or herself known by giving an appropriate sign or signal!"

Wilbur paused and listened. All the other animals lifted their heads and stared at him. Wilbur blushed. But he was determined to get in touch with his unknown friend.

"Attention, please!" he said. "I will repeat the message. Will the party who addressed me at bedtime last night kindly speak up. Please tell me where you are, if you are my friend!"

The sheep looked at each other in disgust.

"Stop your nonsense, Wilbur!" said the oldest sheep. "If you have a new friend here, you are probably disturbing his rest; and the quickest way to spoil a friendship is to wake somebody up in the morning before he is ready. How can you be sure your friend is an early riser?"

"I beg everyone's pardon," whispered Wilbur. "I didn't mean to be objectionable."

He lay down meekly in the manure, facing the door. He did not know it, but his friend was very near. And the old sheep was right—the friend was still asleep.

Soon Lurvy appeared with slops for breakfast. Wilbur rushed out, ate everything in a hurry, and licked the trough. The sheep moved off down the lane, the gander waddled along behind them, pulling grass. And then, just as Wilbur was settling down for his morning nap, he heard again the thin voice that had addressed him the night before.

"Salutations!" said the voice.

Wilbur jumped to his feet. "Salu-*what*?" he cried.

"Salutations!" repeated the voice.

"What are *they*, and where are *you*?" screamed Wilbur. "Please, *please*, tell me where you are. And what are salutations?"

"Salutations are greetings," said the voice. "When I say 'salutations,' it's just my fancy way of saying hello or good morning. Actually, it's a silly expression, and

I am surprised that I used it at all. As for my where-
abouts, that's easy. Look up here in the corner of the
doorway! Here I am. Look, I'm waving!"

At last Wilbur saw the creature that had spoken to
him in such a kindly way. Stretched across the upper
part of the doorway was a big spiderweb, and hanging

from the top of the web, head down, was a large grey spider. She was about the size of a gumdrop. She had eight legs, and she was waving one of them at Wilbur in friendly greeting. "See me now?" she asked.

"Oh, yes indeed," said Wilbur. "Yes indeed! How are you? Good morning! Salutations! Very pleased to meet you. What is your name, please? May I have your name?"

"My name," said the spider, "is Charlotte."

"Charlotte what?" asked Wilbur, eagerly.

"Charlotte A. Cavatica. But just call me Charlotte."

"I think you're beautiful," said Wilbur.

"Well, I *am* pretty," replied Charlotte. "There's no denying that. Almost all spiders are rather nice-looking. I'm not as flashy as some, but I'll do. I wish I could see you, Wilbur, as clearly as you can see me."

"Why can't you?" asked the pig. "I'm right here."

"Yes, but I'm near-sighted," replied Charlotte. "I've always been dreadfully near-sighted. It's good in some ways, not so good in others. Watch me wrap up this fly."

A fly that had been crawling along Wilbur's trough had flown up and blundered into the lower part of Charlotte's web and was tangled in the sticky threads. The fly was beating its wings furiously, trying to break loose and free itself.

"First," said Charlotte, "I dive at him." She plunged

headfirst toward the fly. As she dropped, a tiny silken thread unwound from her rear end.

"Next, I wrap him up." She grabbed the fly, threw a few jets of silk around it, and rolled it over and over, wrapping it so that it couldn't move. Wilbur watched

in horror. He could hardly believe what he was seeing, and although he detested flies, he was sorry for this one.

"There!" said Charlotte. "Now I knock him out, so he'll be more comfortable." She bit the fly. "He can't feel a thing now," she remarked. "He'll make a perfect breakfast for me."

"You mean you *eat* flies?" gasped Wilbur.

"Certainly. Flies, bugs, grasshoppers, choice beetles, moths, butterflies, tasty cockroaches, gnats, midges, daddy longlegs, centipedes, mosquitoes, crickets—anything that is careless enough to get caught in my web. I have to live, don't I?"

"Why, yes, of course," said Wilbur. "Do they taste good?"

"Delicious. Of course, I don't really eat them. I drink them—drink their blood. I love blood," said Charlotte, and her pleasant, thin voice grew even thinner and more pleasant.

"Don't say that!" groaned Wilbur. "Please don't say things like that!"

"Why not? It's true, and I have to say what is true. I am not entirely happy about my diet of flies and bugs, but it's the way I'm made. A spider has to pick up a living somehow or other, and I happen to be a trapper. I just naturally build a web and trap flies and other insects. My mother was a trapper before me. Her mother was a trapper before her. All our family have been trappers. Way back for thousands and thousands of years we spiders have been laying for flies and bugs."

"It's a miserable inheritance," said Wilbur, gloomily. He was sad because his new friend was so bloodthirsty.

"Yes, it is," agreed Charlotte. "But I can't help it. I don't know how the first spider in the early days of the world happened to think up this fancy idea of spinning a web, but she did, and it was clever of her, too. And since then, all of us spiders have had to work the same trick. It's not a bad pitch, on the whole."

"It's cruel," replied Wilbur, who did not intend to be argued out of his position.

"Well, *you* can't talk," said Charlotte. "*You* have your meals brought to you in a pail. Nobody feeds me. I have to get my own living. I live by my wits. I have to be sharp and clever, lest I go hungry. I have to think things out, catch what I can, take what comes. And it just so happens, my friend, that what comes is flies and insects and bugs. And *further*more," said Charlotte, shaking one of her legs, "do you realize that if I didn't catch bugs and eat them, bugs would increase and multiply and get so numerous that they'd destroy the earth, wipe out everything?"

"Really?" said Wilbur. "I wouldn't want *that* to happen. Perhaps your web is a good thing after all."

The goose had been listening to this conversation and chuckling to herself. "There are a lot of things Wilbur doesn't know about life," she thought. "He's really a very innocent little pig. He doesn't even know what's going to happen to him around Christmastime; he has no idea that Mr. Zuckerman and Lurvy are plotting to kill him." And the goose raised herself a bit and poked her eggs a little further under her so that they would receive the full heat from her warm body and soft feathers.

Charlotte stood quietly over the fly, preparing to eat it. Wilbur lay down and closed his eyes. He was tired from his wakeful night and from the excitement of meeting someone for the first time. A breeze brought him the smell of clover—the sweet-smelling world beyond his fence. "Well," he thought, "I've got a new friend, all right. But what a gamble friendship is! Charlotte is fierce, brutal, scheming, bloodthirsty—everything I don't like. How can I learn to like her, even though she is pretty and, of course, clever?"

Wilbur was merely suffering the doubts and fears that often go with finding a new friend. In good time he was to discover that he was mistaken about Charlotte. Underneath her rather bold and cruel exterior, she had a kind heart, and she was to prove loyal and true to the very end.

VI. *Summer Days*

T HE EARLY summer days on a farm are the happiest and fairest days of the year. Lilacs bloom and make the air sweet, and then fade. Apple blossoms come with the lilacs, and the bees visit around among the apple trees. The days grow warm and soft. School ends, and children have time to play and to fish for trouts in the brook. Avery often brought a trout home in his pocket, warm and stiff and ready to be fried for supper.

Now that school was over, Fern visited the barn almost every day, to sit quietly on her stool. The animals treated her as an equal. The sheep lay calmly at her feet.

Around the first of July, the work horses were hitched to the mowing machine, and Mr. Zuckerman climbed into the seat and drove into the field. All morning you could hear the rattle of the machine as it went round and round, while the tall grass fell down behind the cutter bar in long green swathes. Next day, if there was no thunder shower, all hands would help rake and pitch and load, and the hay would be hauled to the barn in the high hay wagon, with Fern and Avery riding at the top of the load. Then the hay would be hoisted, sweet and warm, into the big loft, until the whole barn seemed like a wonderful bed of timothy and clover. It was fine to jump in, and perfect to hide in. And sometimes Avery would find a little grass snake in the hay, and would add it to the other things in his pocket.

Early summer days are a jubilee time for birds. In the fields, around the house, in the barn, in the woods, in the swamp—everywhere love and songs and nests and eggs. From the edge of the woods, the white-throated sparrow (which must come all the way from Boston) calls, "Oh, Peabody, Peabody, Peabody!" On an apple bough, the phoebe teeters and wags its tail and says, "Phoebe, phoe-bee!" The song sparrow, who knows how brief and lovely life is, says, "Sweet, sweet, sweet interlude; sweet, sweet, sweet interlude." If you enter the barn, the swallows swoop down from their nests and scold. "Cheeky, cheeky!" they say.

In early summer there are plenty of things for a child to eat and drink and suck and chew. Dandelion stems are full of milk, clover heads are loaded with nectar, the Frigidaire is full of ice-cold drinks. Everywhere you look is life; even the little ball of spit on the weed stalk, if you poke it apart, has a green worm inside it. And on the under side of the leaf of the potato vine are the bright orange eggs of the potato bug.

It was on a day in early summer that the goose eggs hatched. This was an important event in the barn cellar. Fern was there, sitting on her stool, when it happened.

Except for the goose herself, Charlotte was the first to know that the goslings had at last arrived. The goose knew a day in advance that they were coming—she could hear their weak voices calling from inside the egg. She knew that they were in a desperately cramped position inside the shell and were most anxious to break through and get out. So she sat quite still, and talked less than usual.

When the first gosling poked its grey-green head through the goose's feathers and looked around, Charlotte spied it and made the announcement.

"I am sure," she said, "that every one of us here will be gratified to learn that after four weeks of unremitting effort and patience on the part of our friend the goose, she now has something to show for it. The goslings have arrived. May I offer my sincere congratulations!"

"Thank you, thank you, thank you!" said the goose, nodding and bowing shamelessly.

"Thank you," said the gander.

"Congratulations!" shouted Wilbur. "How many goslings are there? I can only see one."

"There are seven," said the goose.

"Fine!" said Charlotte. "Seven is a lucky number."

"Luck had nothing to do with this," said the goose. "It was good management and hard work."

At this point, Templeton showed his nose from his hiding place under Wilbur's trough. He glanced at Fern, then crept cautiously toward the goose, keeping close to the wall. Everyone watched him, for he was not well liked, not trusted.

"Look," he began in his sharp voice, "you say you have seven goslings. There were eight eggs. What happened to the other egg? Why didn't it hatch?"

"It's a dud, I guess," said the goose.

"What are you going to do with it?" continued Templeton, his little round beady eyes fixed on the goose.

"You can have it," replied the goose. "Roll it away and add it to that nasty collection of yours." (Templeton had a habit of picking up unusual objects around the farm and storing them in his home. He saved everything.)

"Certainly-ertainly-ertainly," said the gander. "You may have the egg. But I'll tell you one thing, Templeton, if I ever catch you poking-oking-oking your ugly nose around our goslings, I'll give you the worst pounding a rat ever took." And the gander opened his strong wings and beat the air with them to show his power. He was strong and brave, but the truth is, both the

goose and the gander were worried about Templeton.
And with good reason. The rat had no morals, no con-
science, no scruples, no consideration, no decency, no
milk of rodent kindness, no compunctions, no higher
feeling, no friendliness, no anything. He would kill a
gosling if he could get away with it—the goose knew
that. Everybody knew it.

With her broad bill the goose pushed the unhatched egg out of the nest, and the entire company watched in disgust while the rat rolled it away. Even Wilbur, who could eat almost anything, was appalled. "Imagine wanting a junky old rotten egg!" he muttered.

"A rat is a rat," said Charlotte. She laughed a tinkling little laugh. "But, my friends, if that ancient egg ever breaks, this barn will be untenable."

"What's that mean?" asked Wilbur.

"It means nobody will be able to live here on account of the smell. A rotten egg is a regular stink bomb."

"I won't break it," snarled Templeton. "I know what I'm doing. I handle stuff like this all the time."

He disappeared into his tunnel, pushing the goose egg in front of him. He pushed and nudged till he succeeded in rolling it to his lair under the trough.

That afternoon, when the wind had died down and the barnyard was quiet and warm, the grey goose led her seven goslings off the nest and out into the world. Mr. Zuckerman spied them when he came with Wilbur's supper.

"Well, hello there!" he said, smiling all over. "Let's see . . . one, two, three, four, five, six, seven. Seven baby geese. Now isn't that lovely!"

VII. *Bad News*

WILBUR liked Charlotte better and better each day. Her campaign against insects seemed sensible and useful. Hardly anybody around the farm had a good word to say for a fly. Flies spent their time pestering others. The cows hated them. The horses detested them. The sheep loathed them. Mr. and Mrs. Zuckerman were always complaining about them, and putting up screens.

Wilbur admired the way Charlotte managed. He was particularly glad that she always put her victim to sleep before eating it.

"It's real thoughtful of you to do that, Charlotte," he said.

"Yes," she replied in her sweet, musical voice, "I always give them an anaesthetic so they won't feel pain. It's a little service I throw in."

As the days went by, Wilbur grew and grew. He ate three big meals a day. He spent long hours lying on his side, half asleep, dreaming pleasant dreams. He enjoyed

good health and he gained a lot of weight. One afternoon, when Fern was sitting on her stool, the oldest
sheep walked into the barn, and stopped to pay a call
on Wilbur.

"Hello!" she said. "Seems to me you're putting on
weight."

"Yes, I guess I am," replied Wilbur. "At my age it's
a good idea to keep gaining."

"Just the same, I don't envy you," said the old sheep.
"You know why they're fattening you up, don't you?"

"No," said Wilbur.

"Well, I don't like to spread bad news," said the
sheep, "but they're fattening you up because they're
going to kill you, that's why."

"They're going to *what*?" screamed Wilbur. Fern
grew rigid on her stool.

"Kill you. Turn you into smoked bacon and ham,"
continued the old sheep. "Almost all young pigs get
murdered by the farmer as soon as the real cold weather
sets in. There's a regular conspiracy around here to kill
you at Christmastime. Everybody is in the plot—
Lurvy, Zuckerman, even John Arable."

"Mr. Arable?" sobbed Wilbur. "Fern's father?"

"Certainly. When a pig is to be butchered, everybody helps. I'm an old sheep and I see the same thing,
same old business, year after year. Arable arrives with
his .22, shoots the . . ."

"Stop!" screamed Wilbur. "I don't want to die! Save me, somebody! Save me!" Fern was just about to jump up when a voice was heard.

"Be quiet, Wilbur!" said Charlotte, who had been listening to this awful conversation.

"I can't be quiet," screamed Wilbur, racing up and down. "I don't want to be killed. I don't want to die. Is it true what the old sheep says, Charlotte? Is it true they are going to kill me when the cold weather comes?"

"Well," said the spider, plucking thoughtfully at her

web, "the old sheep has been around this barn a long time. She has seen many a spring pig come and go. If she says they plan to kill you, I'm sure it's true. It's also the dirtiest trick I ever heard of. What people don't think of!"

Wilbur burst into tears. "I don't *want* to die," he moaned. "I want to stay alive, right here in my comfortable manure pile with all my friends. I want to breathe the beautiful air and lie in the beautiful sun."

"You're certainly making a beautiful noise," snapped the old sheep.

"I don't want to die!" screamed Wilbur, throwing himself to the ground.

"You shall not die," said Charlotte, briskly.

"What? Really?" cried Wilbur. "Who's going to save me?"

"I am," said Charlotte.

"How?" asked Wilbur.

"That remains to be seen. But I am going to save you, and I want you to quiet down immediately. You're carrying on in a childish way. Stop your crying! I can't stand hysterics."

VIII. A Talk at Home

ON SUNDAY morning Mr. and Mrs. Arable and Fern were sitting at breakfast in the kitchen. Avery had finished and was upstairs looking for his slingshot.

"Did you know that Uncle Homer's goslings had hatched?" asked Fern.

"How many?" asked Mr. Arable.

"Seven," replied Fern. "There were eight eggs but one egg didn't hatch and the goose told Templeton she didn't want it any more, so he took it away."

"The goose did what?" asked Mrs. Arable, gazing at her daughter with a queer, worried look.

"Told Templeton she didn't want the egg any more," repeated Fern.

"Who is Templeton?" asked Mrs. Arable.

"He's the rat," replied Fern. "None of us like him much."

"Who's 'us'?" asked Mr. Arable.

"Oh, everybody in the barn cellar. Wilbur and the

sheep and the lambs and the goose and the gander and the goslings and Charlotte and me."

"Charlotte?" said Mrs. Arable. "Who's Charlotte?"

"She's Wilbur's best friend. She's terribly clever."

"What does she look like?" asked Mrs. Arable.

"Well-l," said Fern, thoughtfully, "she has eight legs. All spiders do, I guess."

"Charlotte is a spider?" asked Fern's mother.

Fern nodded. "A big grey one. She has a web across the top of Wilbur's doorway. She catches flies and sucks their blood. Wilbur adores her."

"Does he really?" said Mrs. Arable, rather vaguely. She was staring at Fern with a worried expression on her face.

"Oh, yes, Wilbur adores Charlotte," said Fern. "Do you know what Charlotte said when the goslings hatched?"

"I haven't the faintest idea," said Mr. Arable. "Tell us."

"Well, when the first gosling stuck its little head out from under the goose, I was sitting on my stool in the corner and Charlotte was on her web. She made a speech. She said: 'I am sure that every one of us here in the barn cellar will be gratified to learn that after four weeks of unremitting effort and patience on the part of the goose, she now has something to show for it.' Don't you think that was a pleasant thing for her to say?"

"Yes, I do," said Mrs. Arable. "And now, Fern, it's time to get ready for Sunday School. And tell Avery to get ready. And this afternoon you can tell me more about what goes on in Uncle Homer's barn. Aren't you spending quite a lot of time there? You go there almost every afternoon, don't you?"

"I like it there," replied Fern. She wiped her mouth and ran upstairs. After she had left the room, Mrs. Arable spoke in a low voice to her husband.

"I worry about Fern," she said. "Did you hear the way she rambled on about the animals, pretending that they talked?"

Mr. Arable chuckled. "Maybe they do talk," he said. "I've sometimes wondered. At any rate, don't worry about Fern—she's just got a lively imagination. Kids think they hear all sorts of things."

"Just the same, I *do* worry about her," replied Mrs. Arable. "I think I shall ask Dr. Dorian about her the next time I see him. He loves Fern almost as much as we do, and I want him to know how queerly she is acting about that pig and everything. I don't think it's normal. You know perfectly well animals don't talk."

Mr. Arable grinned. "Maybe our ears aren't as sharp as Fern's," he said.

IX. Wilbur's Boast

ASPIDER'S web is stronger than it looks. Although it is made of thin, delicate strands, the web is not easily broken. However, a web gets torn every day by the insects that kick around in it, and a spider must rebuild it when it gets full of holes. Charlotte liked to do her weaving during the late afternoon, and Fern liked to sit nearby and watch. One afternoon she heard a most interesting conversation and witnessed a strange event.

"You have awfully hairy legs, Charlotte," said Wilbur, as the spider busily worked at her task.

"My legs are hairy for a good reason," replied Charlotte. "Furthermore, each leg of mine has seven sections—the coxa, the trochanter, the femur, the patella, the tibia, the metatarsus, and the tarsus."

Wilbur sat bolt upright. "You're kidding," he said.

"No, I'm not, either."

"Say those names again, I didn't catch them the first time."

"Coxa, trochanter, femur, patella, tibia, metatarsus, and tarsus."

"Goodness!" said Wilbur, looking down at his own chubby legs. "I don't think *my* legs have seven sections."

"Well," said Charlotte, "you and I lead different lives. You don't have to spin a web. That takes real leg work."

"I could spin a web if I tried," said Wilbur, boasting. "I've just never tried."

"Let's see you do it," said Charlotte. Fern chuckled softly, and her eyes grew wide with love for the pig.

"O.K.," replied Wilbur. "You coach me and I'll spin one. It must be a lot of fun to spin a web. How do I start?"

"Take a deep breath!" said Charlotte, smiling. Wilbur breathed deeply. "Now climb to the highest place you can get to, like this." Charlotte raced up to the top of the doorway. Wilbur scrambled to the top of the manure pile.

"Very good!" said Charlotte. "Now make an attachment with your spinnerets, hurl yourself into space, and let out a dragline as you go down!"

Wilbur hesitated a moment, then jumped out into the air. He glanced hastily behind to see if a piece of rope was following him to check his fall, but nothing seemed to be happening in his rear, and the next thing he knew he landed with a thump. "Ooomp!" he grunted.

Charlotte laughed so hard her web began to sway.

"What did I do wrong?" asked the pig, when he recovered from his bump.

"Nothing," said Charlotte. "It was a nice try."

"I think I'll try again," said Wilbur, cheerfully. "I believe what I need is a little piece of string to hold me."

The pig walked out to his yard. "You there, Templeton?" he called. The rat poked his head out from under the trough.

"Got a little piece of string I could borrow?" asked Wilbur. "I need it to spin a web."

"Yes, indeed," replied Templeton, who saved string. "No trouble at all. Anything to oblige." He crept down into his hole, pushed the goose egg out of the way, and returned with an old piece of dirty white string. Wilbur examined it.

"That's just the thing," he said. "Tie one end to my tail, will you, Templeton?"

Wilbur crouched low, with his thin, curly tail toward the rat. Templeton seized the string, passed it around the end of the pig's tail, and tied two half hitches. Charlotte watched in delight. Like Fern, she was truly fond of Wilbur, whose smelly pen and stale food attracted the flies that she needed, and she was proud to see that he was not a quitter and was willing to try again to spin a web.

While the rat and the spider and the little girl watched, Wilbur climbed again to the top of the manure pile, full of energy and hope.

"Everybody watch!" he cried. And summoning all his strength, he threw himself into the air, headfirst. The string trailed behind him. But as he had neglected to fasten the other end to anything, it didn't really do any good, and Wilbur landed with a thud, crushed and hurt. Tears came to his eyes. Templeton grinned. Charlotte just sat quietly. After a bit she spoke.

"You can't spin a web, Wilbur, and I advise you to put the idea out of your mind. You lack two things needed for spinning a web."

"What are they?" asked Wilbur, sadly.

"You lack a set of spinnerets, and you lack know-

how. But cheer up, you don't need a web. Zuckerman supplies you with three big meals a day. Why should you worry about trapping food?"

Wilbur sighed. "You're ever so much cleverer and brighter than I am, Charlotte. I guess I was just trying to show off. Serves me right."

Templeton untied his string and took it back to his home. Charlotte returned to her weaving.

"You needn't feel too badly, Wilbur," she said. "Not many creatures can spin webs. Even men aren't as good at it as spiders, although they *think* they're pretty good, and they'll *try* anything. Did you ever hear of the Queensborough Bridge?"

Wilbur shook his head. "Is it a web?"

"Sort of," replied Charlotte. "But do you know how long it took men to build it? Eight whole years. My goodness, I would have starved to death waiting that long. I can make a web in a single evening."

"What do people catch in the Queensborough Bridge —bugs?" asked Wilbur.

"No," said Charlotte. "They don't catch anything. They just keep trotting back and forth across the bridge thinking there is something better on the other side. If they'd hang head-down at the top of the thing and wait quietly, maybe something good would come along. But no—with men it's rush, rush, rush, every minute. I'm glad I'm a sedentary spider."

"What does sedentary mean?" asked Wilbur.

"Means I sit still a good part of the time and don't go wandering all over creation. I know a good thing when I see it, and my web is a good thing. I stay put and wait for what comes. Gives me a chance to think."

"Well, I'm sort of sedentary myself, I guess," said the pig. "I have to hang around here whether I want to or not. You know where I'd really like to be this evening?"

"Where?"

"In a forest looking for beechnuts and truffles and delectable roots, pushing leaves aside with my wonderful strong nose, searching and sniffing along the ground, smelling, smelling, smelling . . ."

"You smell just the way you are," remarked a lamb who had just walked in. "I can smell you from here. You're the smelliest creature in the place."

Wilbur hung his head. His eyes grew wet with tears. Charlotte noticed his embarrassment and she spoke sharply to the lamb.

"Let Wilbur alone!" she said. "He has a perfect right to smell, considering his surroundings. You're no bundle of sweet peas yourself. Furthermore, you are interrupting a very pleasant conversation. What were we talking about, Wilbur, when we were so rudely interrupted?"

"Oh, I don't remember," said Wilbur. "It doesn't

make any difference. Let's not talk any more for a while, Charlotte. I'm getting sleepy. You go ahead and finish fixing your web and I'll just lie here and watch you. It's a lovely evening." Wilbur stretched out on his side.

Twilight settled over Zuckerman's barn, and a feeling of peace. Fern knew it was almost suppertime but she couldn't bear to leave. Swallows passed on silent wings, in and out of the doorways, bringing food to their young ones. From across the road a bird sang "Whippoorwill, whippoorwill!" Lurvy sat down under an apple tree and lit his pipe; the animals sniffed the familiar smell of strong tobacco. Wilbur heard the trill of the tree toad and the occasional slamming of the kitchen door. All these sounds made him feel comfortable and happy, for he loved life and loved to be a part of the world on a summer evening. But as he lay there he remembered what the old sheep had told him. The thought of death came to him and he began to tremble with fear.

"Charlotte?" he said, softly.

"Yes, Wilbur?"

"I don't want to die."

"Of course you don't," said Charlotte in a comforting voice.

"I just love it here in the barn," said Wilbur. "I love everything about this place."

"Of course you do," said Charlotte. "We all do."

The goose appeared, followed by her seven goslings. They thrust their little necks out and kept up a musical whistling, like a tiny troupe of pipers. Wilbur listened to the sound with love in his heart.

"Charlotte?" he said.

"Yes?" said the spider.

"Were you serious when you promised you would keep them from killing me?"

"I was never more serious in my life. I am not going to let you die, Wilbur."

"How are you going to save me?" asked Wilbur, whose curiosity was very strong on this point.

"Well," said Charlotte, vaguely, "I don't really know. But I'm working on a plan."

"That's wonderful," said Wilbur. "How is the plan coming, Charlotte? Have you got very far with it? Is it coming along pretty well?" Wilbur was trembling again, but Charlotte was cool and collected.

"Oh, it's coming all right," she said, lightly. "The plan is still in its early stages and hasn't completely shaped up yet, but I'm working on it."

"When do you work on it?" begged Wilbur.

"When I'm hanging head-down at the top of my web. That's when I do my thinking, because then all the blood is in my head."

"I'd be only too glad to help in any way I can."

"Oh, I'll work it out alone," said Charlotte. "I can think better if I think alone."

"All right," said Wilbur. "But don't fail to let me know if there's anything I can do to help, no matter how slight."

"Well," replied Charlotte, "you must try to build yourself up. I want you to get plenty of sleep, and stop worrying. Never hurry and never worry! Chew your food thoroughly and eat every bit of it, except you must leave just enough for Templeton. Gain weight and stay well—that's the way you can help. Keep fit, and don't lose your nerve. Do you think you understand?"

"Yes, I understand," said Wilbur.

"Go along to bed, then," said Charlotte. "Sleep is important."

Wilbur trotted over to the darkest corner of his pen and threw himself down. He closed his eyes. In another minute he spoke.

"Charlotte?" he said.

"Yes, Wilbur?"

"May I go out to my trough and see if I left any of my supper? I think I left just a tiny bit of mashed potato."

"Very well," said Charlotte. "But I want you in bed again without delay."

Wilbur started to race out to his yard.

"Slowly, slowly!" said Charlotte. "Never hurry and never worry!"

Wilbur checked himself and crept slowly to his trough. He found a bit of potato, chewed it carefully, swallowed it, and walked back to bed. He closed his eyes and was silent for a while.

"Charlotte?" he said, in a whisper.

"Yes?"

"May I get a drink of milk? I think there are a few drops of milk left in my trough."

"No, the trough is dry, and I want you to go to sleep. No more talking! Close your eyes and go to sleep!"

Wilbur shut his eyes. Fern got up from her stool and started for home, her mind full of everything she had seen and heard.

"Good night, Charlotte!" said Wilbur.

"Good night, Wilbur!"

There was a pause.

"Good night, Charlotte!"

"Good night, Wilbur!"

"Good night!"

"Good night!"

X. An Explosion

DAY AFTER day the spider waited, head-down, for an idea to come to her. Hour by hour she sat motionless, deep in thought. Having promised Wilbur that she would save his life, she was determined to keep her promise. Charlotte was naturally patient. She knew from experience that if she waited long enough, a fly would come to her web; and she felt sure that if she thought long enough about Wilbur's problem, an idea would come to her mind.

Finally, one morning toward the middle of July, the idea came. "Why, how perfectly simple!" she said to herself. "The way to save Wilbur's life is to play a trick on Zuckerman. If I can fool a bug," thought Charlotte, "I can surely fool a man. People are not as smart as bugs."

Wilbur walked into his yard just at that moment.

"What are you thinking about, Charlotte?" he asked.

"I was just thinking," said the spider, "that people are very gullible."

"What does 'gullible' mean?"

"Easy to fool," said Charlotte.

"That's a mercy," replied Wilbur, and he lay down in the shade of his fence and went fast asleep. The spider, however, stayed wide awake, gazing affectionately at him and making plans for his future. Summer was half gone. She knew she didn't have much time.

That morning, just as Wilbur fell asleep, Avery Arable wandered into the Zuckerman's front yard, followed by Fern. Avery carried a live frog in his hand.

Fern had a crown of daisies in her hair. The children ran for the kitchen.

"Just in time for a piece of blueberry pie," said Mrs. Zuckerman.

"Look at my frog!" said Avery, placing the frog on the drainboard and holding out his hand for pie.

"Take that thing out of here!" said Mrs. Zuckerman.

"He's hot," said Fern. "He's almost dead, that frog."

"He is not," said Avery. "He lets me scratch him between the eyes." The frog jumped and landed in Mrs. Zuckerman's dishpan full of soapy water.

"You're getting your pie on you," said Fern. "Can I look for eggs in the henhouse, Aunt Edith?"

"Run outdoors, both of you! And don't bother the hens!"

"It's getting all over everything," shouted Fern. "His pie is all over his front."

"Come on, frog!" cried Avery. He scooped up his frog. The frog kicked, splashing soapy water onto the blueberry pie.

"Another crisis!" groaned Fern.

"Let's swing in the swing!" said Avery.

The children ran to the barn.

Mr. Zuckerman had the best swing in the county. It was a single long piece of heavy rope tied to the beam over the north doorway. At the bottom end of the rope was a fat knot to sit on. It was arranged so that you could swing without being pushed. You climbed a ladder to the hayloft. Then, holding the rope, you stood at the edge and looked down, and were scared and dizzy. Then you straddled the knot, so that it acted as a seat. Then you got up all your nerve, took a deep breath, and jumped. For a second you seemed to be falling to the barn floor far below, but then suddenly the rope would begin to catch you, and you would sail through the barn door going a mile a minute, with the wind whistling in your eyes and ears and hair. Then you would zoom upward into the sky, and look up at the clouds, and the rope would twist and you would twist and turn with the rope. Then you would drop down, down, down out of the sky and come sailing back into the barn almost into the hayloft, then sail out again (not quite so far this time), then in again (not quite so high), then out again, then in again, then out, then in; and then you'd jump off and fall down and let somebody else try it.

Mothers for miles around worried about Zuckerman's swing. They feared some child would fall off. But no child ever did. Children almost always hang onto things tighter than their parents think they will.

Avery put the frog in his pocket and climbed to the hayloft. "The last time I swang in this swing, I almost crashed into a barn swallow," he yelled.

"Take that frog out!" ordered Fern.

Avery straddled the rope and jumped. He sailed out through the door, frog and all, and into the sky, frog and all. Then he sailed back into the barn.

"Your tongue is purple!" screamed Fern.

"So is yours!" cried Avery, sailing out again with the frog.

"I have hay inside my dress! It itches!" called Fern.

"Scratch it!" yelled Avery, as he sailed back.

"It's my turn," said Fern. "Jump off!"

"Fern's got the itch!" sang Avery.

When he jumped off, he threw the swing up to his sister. She shut her eyes tight and jumped. She felt the dizzy drop, then the supporting lift of the swing. When she opened her eyes she was looking up into the blue sky and was about to fly back through the door.

They took turns for an hour.

When the children grew tired of swinging, they went down toward the pasture and picked wild raspberries and ate them. Their tongues turned from purple to red. Fern bit into a raspberry that had a bad-tasting bug inside it, and got discouraged. Avery found an empty candy box and put his frog in it. The frog seemed tired after his morning in the swing. The children walked slowly up toward the barn. They, too, were tired and hardly had energy enough to walk.

"Let's build a tree house," suggested Avery. "I want to live in a tree, with my frog."

"I'm going to visit Wilbur," Fern announced.

They climbed the fence into the lane and walked
lazily toward the pigpen. Wilbur heard them coming
and got up.

Avery noticed the spider web, and, coming closer,
he saw Charlotte.

"Hey, look at that big spider!" he said. "It's tre-menjus."

"Leave it alone!" commanded Fern. "You've got a frog—isn't that enough?"

"That's a fine spider and I'm going to capture it," said Avery. He took the cover off the candy box. Then he picked up a stick. "I'm going to knock that ol' spider into this box," he said.

Wilbur's heart almost stopped when he saw what was going on. This might be the end of Charlotte if the boy succeeded in catching her.

"You stop it, Avery!" cried Fern.

Avery put one leg over the fence of the pigpen. He was just about to raise his stick to hit Charlotte when he lost his balance. He swayed and toppled and landed on the edge of Wilbur's trough. The trough tipped up and then came down with a slap. The goose egg was right underneath. There was a dull explosion as the egg broke, and then a horrible smell.

Fern screamed. Avery jumped to his feet. The air was filled with the terrible gases and smells from the rotten egg. Templeton, who had been resting in his home, scuttled away into the barn.

"Good *night*!" screamed Avery. "Good *night*! What a stink! Let's get out of here!"

Fern was crying. She held her nose and ran toward the house. Avery ran after her, holding his nose.

Charlotte felt greatly relieved to see him go. It had been a narrow escape.

Later on that morning, the animals came up from the pasture—the sheep, the lambs, the gander, the goose, and the seven goslings. There were many complaints

about the awful smell, and Wilbur had to tell the story over and over again, of how the Arable boy had tried to capture Charlotte, and how the smell of the broken egg drove him away just in time. "It was that rotten goose egg that saved Charlotte's life," said Wilbur.

The goose was proud of her share in the adventure.

"I'm delighted that the egg never hatched," she gabbled.

Templeton, of course, was miserable over the loss of his beloved egg. But he couldn't resist boasting. "It pays to save things," he said in his surly voice. "A rat never knows when something is going to come in handy. I never throw anything away."

"Well," said one of the lambs, "this whole business is all well and good for Charlotte, but what about the rest of us? The smell is unbearable. Who wants to live in a barn that is perfumed with rotten egg?"

"Don't worry, you'll get used to it," said Templeton. He sat up and pulled wisely at his long whiskers, then crept away to pay a visit to the dump.

When Lurvy showed up at lunchtime carrying a pail of food for Wilbur, he stopped short a few paces from the pigpen. He sniffed the air and made a face.

"What in thunder?" he said. Setting the pail down, he picked up the stick that Avery had dropped and pried the trough up. "Rats!" he said. "Fhew! I might a' known a rat would make a nest under this trough. How I hate a rat!"

And Lurvy dragged Wilbur's trough across the yard and kicked some dirt into the rat's nest, burying the broken egg and all Templeton's other possessions. Then he picked up the pail. Wilbur stood in the trough, drooling with hunger. Lurvy poured. The slops ran creamily down around the pig's eyes and ears. Wilbur grunted. He gulped and sucked, and sucked and gulped, making swishing and swooshing noises, anxious to get everything at once. It was a delicious meal— skim milk, wheat middlings, leftover pancakes, half a doughnut, the rind of a summer squash, two pieces of stale toast, a third of a gingersnap, a fish tail, one orange peel, several noodles from a noodle soup, the scum off a cup of cocoa, an ancient jelly roll, a strip of paper from the lining of the garbage pail, and a spoonful of raspberry jello.

Wilbur ate heartily. He planned to leave half a noodle and a few drops of milk for Templeton. Then he remembered that the rat had been useful in saving Charlotte's life, and that Charlotte was trying to save *his* life. So he left a whole noodle, instead of a half.

Now that the broken egg was buried, the air cleared and the barn smelled good again. The afternoon passed, and evening came. Shadows lengthened. The cool and kindly breath of evening entered through doors and windows. Astride her web, Charlotte sat moodily eating a horsefly and thinking about the future. After a while she bestirred herself.

She descended to the center of the web and there she began to cut some of her lines. She worked slowly but steadily while the other creatures drowsed. None of the others, not even the goose, noticed that she was at work. Deep in his soft bed, Wilbur snoozed. Over in their favorite corner, the goslings whistled a night song.

Charlotte tore quite a section out of her web, leaving an open space in the middle. Then she started weaving something to take the place of the threads she had removed. When Templeton got back from the dump, around midnight, the spider was still at work.

XI. The Miracle

THE NEXT day was foggy. Everything on the farm was dripping wet. The grass looked like a magic carpet. The asparagus patch looked like a silver forest.

On foggy mornings, Charlotte's web was truly a thing of beauty. This morning each thin strand was decorated with dozens of tiny beads of water. The web glistened in the light and made a pattern of loveliness and mystery, like a delicate veil. Even Lurvy, who wasn't particularly interested in beauty, noticed the web when he came with the pig's breakfast. He noted how clearly it showed up and he noted how big and carefully built it was. And then he took another look and he saw something that made him set his pail down. There, in the center of the web, neatly woven in block letters, was a message. It said:

SOME PIG!

Lurvy felt weak. He brushed his hand across his eyes and stared harder at Charlotte's web.

"I'm seeing things," he whispered. He dropped to his knees and uttered a short prayer. Then, forgetting all about Wilbur's breakfast, he walked back to the house and called Mr. Zuckerman.

"I think you'd better come down to the pigpen," he said.

"What's the trouble?" asked Mr. Zuckerman. "Anything wrong with the pig?"

"N-not exactly," said Lurvy. "Come and see for yourself."

The two men walked silently down to Wilbur's yard. Lurvy pointed to the spider's web. "Do you see what I see?" he asked.

Zuckerman stared at the writing on the web. Then he murmured the words "Some Pig." Then he looked at Lurvy. Then they both began to tremble. Charlotte, sleepy after her night's exertions, smiled as she watched. Wilbur came and stood directly under the web.

"Some pig!" muttered Lurvy in a low voice.

"Some pig!" whispered Mr. Zuckerman. They stared and stared for a long time at Wilbur. Then they stared at Charlotte.

"You don't suppose that that spider . . ." began Mr. Zuckerman—but he shook his head and didn't finish the sentence. Instead, he walked solemnly back up to the house and spoke to his wife. "Edith, something has happened," he said, in a weak voice. He went into the living room and sat down, and Mrs. Zuckerman followed.

"I've got something to tell you, Edith," he said. "You better sit down."

Mrs. Zuckerman sank into a chair. She looked pale and frightened.

"Edith," he said, trying to keep his voice steady, "I think you had best be told that we have a very unusual pig."

A look of complete bewilderment came over Mrs. Zuckerman's face. "Homer Zuckerman, what in the world are you talking about?" she said.

"This is a very serious thing, Edith," he replied. "Our pig is completely out of the ordinary."

"What's unusual about the pig?" asked Mrs. Zuckerman, who was beginning to recover from her scare.

"Well, I don't really know yet," said Mr. Zuckerman. "But we have received a sign, Edith—a mysterious sign. A miracle has happened on this farm. There is a large spider's web in the doorway of the barn cellar, right over the pigpen, and when Lurvy went to feed the pig this morning, he noticed the web because it was foggy, and you know how a spider's web looks very distinct in a fog. And right spang in the middle of the web there were the words 'Some Pig.' The words were woven right into the web. They were actually part of the web, Edith. I know, because I have been down there and seen them. It says, 'Some Pig,' just as clear as clear can be. There can be no mistake about it. A miracle has happened and a sign has occurred here on earth, right on our farm, and we have no ordinary pig."

"Well," said Mrs. Zuckerman, "it seems to me you're a little off. It seems to me we have no ordinary *spider*."

"Oh, no," said Zuckerman. "It's the pig that's un-usual. It says so, right there in the middle of the web."

"Maybe so," said Mrs. Zuckerman. "Just the same, I intend to have a look at that spider."

"It's just a common grey spider," said Zuckerman.

They got up, and together they walked down to Wilbur's yard. "You see, Edith? It's just a common grey spider."

Wilbur was pleased to receive so much attention. Lurvy was still standing there, and Mr. and Mrs. Zuckerman, all three, stood for about an hour, reading the words on the web over and over, and watching Wilbur.

Charlotte was delighted with the way her trick was working. She sat without moving a muscle, and lis-tened to the conversation of the people. When a small fly blundered into the web, just beyond the word "pig," Charlotte dropped quickly down, rolled the fly up, and carried it out of the way.

After a while the fog lifted. The web dried off and the words didn't show up so plainly. The Zuckermans and Lurvy walked back to the house. Just before they left the pigpen, Mr. Zuckerman took one last look at Wilbur.

"You know," he said, in an important voice, "I've thought all along that that pig of ours was an extra good one. He's a solid pig. That pig is as solid as they come.

You notice how solid he is around the shoulders, Lurvy?"

"Sure. Sure I do," said Lurvy. "I've always noticed that pig. He's quite a pig."

"He's long, and he's smooth," said Zuckerman.

"That's right," agreed Lurvy. "He's as smooth as they come. He's some pig."

When Mr. Zuckerman got back to the house, he took off his work clothes and put on his best suit. Then he got into his car and drove to the minister's house. He stayed for an hour and explained to the minister that a miracle had happened on the farm.

"So far," said Zuckerman, "only four people on earth know about this miracle—myself, my wife Edith, my hired man Lurvy, and you."

"Don't tell anybody else," said the minister. "We don't know what it means yet, but perhaps if I give thought to it, I can explain it in my sermon next Sunday. There can be no doubt that you have a most unusual pig. I intend to speak about it in my sermon and point out the fact that this community has been visited with a wondrous animal. By the way, does the pig have a name?"

"Why, yes," said Mr. Zuckerman. "My little niece calls him Wilbur. She's a rather queer child—full of notions. She raised the pig on a bottle and I bought him from her when he was a month old."

He shook hands with the minister, and left.

Secrets are hard to keep. Long before Sunday came, the news spread all over the county. Everybody knew

that a sign had appeared in a spider's web on the Zuckerman place. Everybody knew that the Zuckermans had a wondrous pig. People came from miles around to look at Wilbur and to read the words on Charlotte's web. The Zuckermans' driveway was full of cars and trucks from morning till night—Fords and Chevvies and Buick roadmasters and GMC pickups and Plymouths and Studebakers and Packards and De Sotos with gyromatic transmissions and Oldsmobiles with rocket engines and Jeep station wagons and Pontiacs. The news of the wonderful pig spread clear up into the hills, and farmers came rattling down in buggies and buckboards, to stand hour after hour at Wilbur's pen admiring the miraculous animal. All said they had never seen such a pig before in their lives.

When Fern told her mother that Avery had tried to hit the Zuckermans' spider with a stick, Mrs. Arable was so shocked that she sent Avery to bed without any supper, as punishment.

In the days that followed, Mr. Zuckerman was so busy entertaining visitors that he neglected his farm work. He wore his good clothes all the time now—got right into them when he got up in the morning. Mrs. Zuckerman prepared special meals for Wilbur. Lurvy shaved and got a haircut; and his principal farm duty was to feed the pig while people looked on.

Mr. Zuckerman ordered Lurvy to increase Wilbur's feedings from three meals a day to four meals a day. The Zuckermans were so busy with visitors they forgot about other things on the farm. The blackberries got ripe, and Mrs. Zuckerman failed to put up any blackberry jam. The corn needed hoeing, and Lurvy didn't find time to hoe it.

On Sunday the church was full. The minister explained the miracle. He said that the words on the spider's web proved that human beings must always be on the watch for the coming of wonders.

All in all, the Zuckermans' pigpen was the center of attraction. Fern was happy, for she felt that Charlotte's trick was working and that Wilbur's life would be saved. But she found that the barn was not nearly as pleasant—too many people. She liked it better when she could be all alone with her friends the animals.

XII. A Meeting

ONE EVENING, a few days after the writing had appeared in Charlotte's web, the spider called a meeting of all the animals in the barn cellar.

"I shall begin by calling the roll. Wilbur?"

"Here!" said the pig.

"Gander?"

"Here, here, here!" said the gander.

"You sound like three ganders," muttered Charlotte. "Why can't you just say 'here'? Why do you have to repeat everything?"

"It's my idio-idio-idiosyncrasy," replied the gander.

"Goose?" said Charlotte.

"Here, here, here!" said the goose. Charlotte glared at her.

"Goslings, one through seven?"

"Bee-bee-bee!" "Bee-bee-bee!" "Bee-bee-bee!" "Bee-bee-bee!" "Bee-bee-bee!" "Bee-bee-bee!" "Bee-bee-bee!" said the goslings.

"This is getting to be quite a meeting," said Charlotte.

"Anybody would think we had three ganders, three geese, and twenty-one goslings. Sheep?"

"He-aa-aa!" answered the sheep all together.

"Lambs?"

"He-aa-aa!" answered the lambs all together.

"Templeton?"

No answer.

"Templeton?"

No answer.

"Well, we are all here except the rat," said Charlotte. "I guess we can proceed without him. Now, all of you must have noticed what's been going on around here the last few days. The message I wrote in my web, praising Wilbur, has been received. The Zuckermans have fallen for it, and so has everybody else. Zuckerman thinks Wilbur is an unusual pig, and therefore he won't want to kill him and eat him. I dare say my trick will work and Wilbur's life can be saved.

"Hurray!" cried everybody.

"Thank you very much," said Charlotte. "Now I called this meeting in order to get suggestions. I need new ideas for the web. People are already getting sick of reading the words 'Some Pig!' If anybody can think of another message, or remark, I'll be glad to weave it into the web. Any suggestions for a new slogan?"

"How about 'Pig Supreme'?" asked one of the lambs.

"No good," said Charlotte. "It sounds like a rich dessert."

"How about 'Terrific, terrific, terrific'?" asked the goose.

"Cut that down to one 'terrific' and it will do very

nicely," said Charlotte. "I think 'terrific' might impress Zuckerman."

"But Charlotte," said Wilbur, "I'm *not* terrific."

"That doesn't make a particle of difference," replied Charlotte. "Not a particle. People believe almost anything they see in print. Does anybody here know how to spell 'terrific'?"

"I think," said the gander, "it's tee double ee double rr double rr double eye double ff double eye double see see see see see."

"What kind of an acrobat do you think I am?" said Charlotte in disgust. "I would have to have St. Vitus's Dance to weave a word like that into my web."

"Sorry, sorry, sorry," said the gander.

Then the oldest sheep spoke up. "I agree that there should be something new written in the web if Wilbur's life is to be saved. And if Charlotte needs help in finding words, I think she can get it from our friend Templeton. The rat visits the dump regularly and has access to old magazines. He can tear out bits of advertisements and bring them up here to the barn cellar, so that Charlotte can have something to copy."

"Good idea," said Charlotte. "But I'm not sure Templeton will be willing to help. You know how he is—always looking out for himself, never thinking of the other fellow."

"I bet I can get him to help," said the old sheep. "I'll

appeal to his baser instincts, of which he has plenty. Here he comes now. Everybody keep quiet while I put the matter up to him!"

The rat entered the barn the way he always did—creeping along close to the wall.

"What's up?" he asked, seeing the animals assembled.

"We're holding a directors' meeting," replied the old sheep.

"Well, break it up!" said Templeton. "Meetings bore me." And the rat began to climb a rope that hung against the wall.

"Look," said the old sheep, "next time you go to the dump, Templeton, bring back a clipping from a magazine. Charlotte needs new ideas so she can write messages in her web and save Wilbur's life."

"Let him die," said the rat. "I should worry."

"You'll worry all right when next winter comes," said the sheep. "You'll worry all right on a zero morning next January when Wilbur is dead and nobody comes down here with a nice pail of warm slops to pour into the trough. Wilbur's leftover food is your chief source of supply, Templeton. *You* know that. Wilbur's food is your food; therefore Wilbur's destiny and your destiny are closely linked. If Wilbur is killed and his trough stands empty day after day, you'll grow so thin we can look right through your stomach and see objects on the other side."

Templeton's whiskers quivered.

"Maybe you're right," he said gruffly. "I'm making a trip to the dump tomorrow afternoon. I'll bring back a magazine clipping if I can find one."

"Thanks," said Charlotte. "The meeting is now adjourned. I have a busy evening ahead of me. I've got to tear my web apart and write 'Terrific.' "

Wilbur blushed. "But I'm *not* terrific, Charlotte. I'm just about average for a pig."

"You're terrific as far as *I'm* concerned," replied Charlotte, sweetly, "and that's what counts. You're my best friend, and *I* think you're sensational. Now stop arguing and go get some sleep!"

XIII. *Good Progress*

AR INTO the night, while the other creatures slept, Charlotte worked on her web. First she ripped out a few of the orb lines near the center. She left the radial lines alone, as they were needed for support. As she worked, her eight legs were a great help to her. So were her teeth. She loved to weave and she was an expert at it. When she was finished ripping things out, her web looked something like this:

A spider can produce several kinds of thread. She uses a dry, tough thread for foundation lines, and she uses a sticky thread for snare lines—the ones that catch and hold insects. Charlotte decided to use her dry thread for writing the new message.

"If I write the word 'Terrific' with sticky thread," she thought, "every bug that comes along will get stuck in it and spoil the effect."

"Now let's see, the first letter is T."

Charlotte climbed to a point at the top of the left hand side of the web. Swinging her spinnerets into position, she attached her thread and then dropped down. As she dropped, her spinning tubes went into action and she let out thread. At the bottom, she attached the thread. This formed the upright part of the letter T. Charlotte was not satisfied, however. She climbed up and made another attachment, right next to the first. Then she carried the line down, so that she had a double line instead of a single line. "It will show up better if I make the whole thing with double lines."

She climbed back up, moved over about an inch to the left, touched her spinnerets to the web, and then carried a line across to the right, forming the top of the T. She repeated this, making it double. Her eight legs were very busy helping.

"Now for the E!"

Charlotte got so interested in her work, she began to

talk to herself, as though to cheer herself on. If you had been sitting quietly in the barn cellar that evening, you would have heard something like this:

"Now for the R! Up we go! Attach! Descend! Pay out line! Whoa! Attach! Good! Up you go! Repeat! Attach! Descend! Pay out line. Whoa, girl! Steady now! Attach! Climb! Attach! Over to the right! Pay out line! Attach! Now right and down and swing that loop and around and around! Now in to the left! Attach! Climb! Repeat! O.K.! Easy, keep those lines together! Now, then, out and down for the leg of the R! Pay out line! Whoa! Attach! Ascend! Repeat! Good girl!"

And so, talking to herself, the spider worked at her difficult task. When it was completed, she felt hungry. She ate a small bug that she had been saving. Then she slept.

Next morning, Wilbur arose and stood beneath the web. He breathed the morning air into his lungs. Drops of dew, catching the sun, made the web stand out clearly. When Lurvy arrived with breakfast, there was the handsome pig, and over him, woven neatly in block letters, was the word TERRIFIC. Another miracle.

Lurvy rushed and called Mr. Zuckerman. Mr. Zuckerman rushed and called Mrs. Zuckerman. Mrs. Zuckerman ran to the phone and called the Arables. The Arables climbed into their truck and hurried over.

Everybody stood at the pigpen and stared at the web and read the word, over and over, while Wilbur, who really *felt* terrific, stood quietly swelling out his chest and swinging his snout from side to side.

"Terrific!" breathed Zuckerman, in joyful admiration. "Edith, you better phone the reporter on the *Weekly Chronicle* and tell him what has happened. He will want to know about this. He may want to bring a photographer. There isn't a pig in the whole state that is as terrific as our pig."

The news spread. People who had journeyed to see Wilbur when he was "some pig" came back again to see him now that he was "terrific."

That afternoon, when Mr. Zuckerman went to milk the cows and clean out the tie-ups, he was still thinking about what a wondrous pig he owned.

"Lurvy!" he called. "There is to be no more cow manure thrown down into that pigpen. I have a terrific pig. I want that pig to have clean, bright straw every day for his bedding. Understand?"

"Yes, sir," said Lurvy.

"Furthermore," said Mr. Zuckerman, "I want you to start building a crate for Wilbur. I have decided to take the pig to the County Fair on September sixth. Make the crate large and paint it green with gold letters!"

"What will the letters say?" asked Lurvy.

"They should say *Zuckerman's Famous Pig.*"

Lurvy picked up a pitchfork and walked away to get some clean straw. Having such an important pig was going to mean plenty of extra work, he could see that.

Below the apple orchard, at the end of a path, was the dump where Mr. Zuckerman threw all sorts of trash and stuff that nobody wanted any more. Here, in a small clearing hidden by young alders and wild raspberry bushes, was an astonishing pile of old bottles and empty tin cans and dirty rags and bits of metal and broken bottles and broken hinges and broken springs and dead batteries and last month's magazines and old discarded dishmops and tattered overalls and rusty spikes and leaky pails and forgotten stoppers and useless junk of all kinds, including a wrong-size crank for a broken ice-cream freezer.

Templeton knew the dump and liked it. There were good hiding places there—excellent cover for a rat. And there was usually a tin can with food still clinging to the inside.

Templeton was down there now, rummaging around. When he returned to the barn, he carried in his mouth an advertisement he had torn from a crumpled magazine.

"How's this?" he asked, showing the ad to Charlotte.

"It says 'Crunchy.' 'Crunchy' would be a good word to write in your web."

"Just the wrong idea," replied Charlotte. "Couldn't be worse. We don't want Zuckerman to think Wilbur is crunchy. He might start thinking about crisp,

crunchy bacon and tasty ham. That would put ideas into his head. We must advertise Wilbur's noble qualities, not his tastiness. Go get another word, please, Templeton!"

The rat looked disgusted. But he sneaked away to the dump and was back in a while with a strip of cotton cloth. "How's this?" he asked. "It's a label off an old shirt."

Charlotte examined the label. It said PRE-SHRUNK.

"I'm sorry, Templeton," she said, "but 'Pre-shrunk' is out of the question. We want Zuckerman to think Wilbur is nicely filled out, not all shrunk up. I'll have to ask you to try again."

"What do you think I am, a messenger boy?" grumbled the rat. "I'm not going to spend all my time chasing down to the dump after advertising material."

"Just once more—please!" said Charlotte.

"I'll tell you what I'll do," said Templeton. "I know where there's a package of soap flakes in the woodshed. It has writing on it. I'll bring you a piece of the package."

He climbed the rope that hung on the wall and disappeared through a hole in the ceiling. When he came back he had a strip of blue-and-white cardboard in his teeth.

"There!" he said, triumphantly. "How's that?"

Charlotte read the words: "With New Radiant Action."

"What does it mean?" asked Charlotte, who had never used any soap flakes in her life.

"How should I know?" said Templeton. "You asked for words and I brought them. I suppose the next thing you'll want me to fetch is a dictionary."

Together they studied the soap ad. " 'With new radiant action,' " repeated Charlotte, slowly. "Wilbur!" she called.

Wilbur, who was asleep in the straw, jumped up.

"Run around!" commanded Charlotte. "I want to see you in action, to see if you are radiant."

Wilbur raced to the end of his yard.

"Now back again, faster!" said Charlotte.

Wilbur galloped back. His skin shone. His tail had a fine, tight curl in it.

"Jump into the air!" cried Charlotte.

Wilbur jumped as high as he could.

"Keep your knees straight and touch the ground with your ears!" called Charlotte.

Wilbur obeyed.

"Do a back flip with a half twist in it!" cried Charlotte.

Wilbur went over backwards, writhing and twisting as he went.

"O.K., Wilbur," said Charlotte. "You can go back to sleep. O.K., Templeton, the soap ad will do, I guess. I'm not sure Wilbur's action is exactly radiant, but it's interesting."

"Actually," said Wilbur, "I *feel* radiant."

"Do you?" said Charlotte, looking at him with affection. "Well, you're a good little pig, and radiant you shall be. I'm in this thing pretty deep now—I might as well go the limit."

Tired from his romp, Wilbur lay down in the clean straw. He closed his eyes. The straw seemed scratchy —not as comfortable as the cow manure, which was always delightfully soft to lie in. So he pushed the straw to one side and stretched out in the manure. Wilbur sighed. It had been a busy day—his first day of being terrific. Dozens of people had visited his yard during the afternoon, and he had had to stand and pose, looking as terrific as he could. Now he was tired. Fern had arrived and seated herself quietly on her stool in the corner.

"Tell me a story, Charlotte!" said Wilbur, as he lay waiting for sleep to come. "Tell me a story!"

So Charlotte, although she, too, was tired, did what Wilbur wanted.

"Once upon a time," she began, "I had a beautiful cousin who managed to build her web across a small stream. One day a tiny fish leaped into the air and got tangled in the web. My cousin was very much surprised, of course. The fish was thrashing wildly. My

cousin hardly dared tackle it. But she did. She swooped down and threw great masses of wrapping material around the fish and fought bravely to capture it."

"Did she succeed?" asked Wilbur.

"It was a never-to-be-forgotten battle," said Charlotte. "There was the fish, caught only by one fin, and its tail wildly thrashing and shining in the sun. There was the web, sagging dangerously under the weight of the fish."

"How much did the fish weigh?" asked Wilbur eagerly.

"I don't know," said Charlotte. "There was my cousin, slipping in, dodging out, beaten mercilessly over the head by the wildly thrashing fish, dancing in, dancing out, throwing her threads and fighting hard. First she threw a left around the tail. The fish lashed back. Then a left to the tail and a right to the mid-section. The fish lashed back. Then she dodged to one side and threw a right, and another right to the fin. Then a hard left to the head, while the web swayed and stretched."

"Then what happened?" asked Wilbur.

"Nothing," said Charlotte. "The fish lost the fight. My cousin wrapped it up so tight it couldn't budge."

"Then what happened?" asked Wilbur.

"Nothing," said Charlotte. "My cousin kept the fish for a while, and then, when she got good and ready, she ate it."

"Tell me another story!" begged Wilbur.

So Charlotte told him about another cousin of hers who was an aeronaut.

"What is an aeronaut?" asked Wilbur.

"A balloonist," said Charlotte. "My cousin used to stand on her head and let out enough thread to form a balloon. Then she'd let go and be lifted into the air and carried upward on the warm wind."

"Is that true?" asked Wilbur. "Or are you just making it up?"

"It's true," replied Charlotte. "I have some very remarkable cousins. And now, Wilbur, it's time you went to sleep."

"Sing something!" begged Wilbur, closing his eyes.

So Charlotte sang a lullaby, while crickets chirped in the grass and the barn grew dark. This was the song she sang.

> "Sleep, sleep, my love, my only,
> Deep, deep, in the dung and the dark;
> Be not afraid and be not lonely!
> This is the hour when frogs and thrushes
> Praise the world from the woods and the rushes.
> Rest from care, my one and only,
> Deep in the dung and the dark!"

But Wilbur was already asleep. When the song ended, Fern got up and went home.

XIV. Dr. Dorian

T HE NEXT day was Saturday. Fern stood at the kitchen sink drying the breakfast dishes as her mother washed them. Mrs. Arable worked silently. She hoped Fern would go out and play with other children, instead of heading for the Zuckermans' barn to sit and watch animals.

"Charlotte is the best storyteller I ever heard," said Fern, poking her dish towel into a cereal bowl.

"Fern," said her mother sternly, "you must not invent things. You know spiders don't tell stories. Spiders can't talk."

"Charlotte can," replied Fern. "She doesn't talk very loud, but she talks."

"What kind of story did she tell?" asked Mrs. Arable.

"Well," began Fern, "she told us about a cousin of hers who caught a fish in her web. Don't you think that's fascinating?"

"Fern, dear, how would a fish get in a spider's web?" said Mrs. Arable. "You know it couldn't happen. You're making this up."

"Oh, it happened all right," replied Fern. "Charlotte never fibs. This cousin of hers built a web across a stream. One day she was hanging around on the web and a tiny fish leaped into the air and got tangled in the web. The fish was caught by one fin, Mother; its tail was wildly thrashing and shining in the sun. Can't you just see the web, sagging dangerously under the weight of the fish? Charlotte's cousin kept slipping in, dodging out, and she was beaten mercilessly over the head by the wildly thrashing fish, dancing in, dancing out, throwing . . ."

"Fern!" snapped her mother. "Stop it! Stop inventing these wild tales!"

"I'm not inventing," said Fern. "I'm just telling you the facts."

"What finally happened?" asked her mother, whose curiosity began to get the better of her.

"Charlotte's cousin won. She wrapped the fish up, then she ate him when she got good and ready. Spiders have to eat, the same as the rest of us."

"Yes, I suppose they do," said Mrs. Arable, vaguely.

"Charlotte has another cousin who is a balloonist. She stands on her head, lets out a lot of line, and is carried aloft on the wind. Mother, wouldn't you simply love to do that?"

"Yes, I would, come to think of it," replied Mrs. Arable. "But Fern, darling, I wish you would play outdoors today instead of going to Uncle Homer's barn. Find some of your playmates and do something nice outdoors. You're spending too much time in that barn —it isn't good for you to be alone so much."

"Alone?" said Fern. "Alone? My best friends are in the barn cellar. It is a very sociable place. Not at all lonely."

Fern disappeared after a while, walking down the road toward Zuckermans'. Her mother dusted the sitting room. As she worked she kept thinking about Fern. It didn't seem natural for a little girl to be so interested in animals. Finally Mrs. Arable made up her mind she would pay a call on old Doctor Dorian and ask his advice. She got in the car and drove to his office in the village.

Dr. Dorian had a thick beard. He was glad to see Mrs. Arable and gave her a comfortable chair.

"It's about Fern," she explained. "Fern spends entirely too much time in the Zuckermans' barn. It doesn't seem normal. She sits on a milk stool in a corner of the barn cellar, near the pigpen, and watches animals, hour after hour. She just sits and listens."

Dr. Dorian leaned back and closed his eyes.

"How enchanting!" he said. "It must be real nice and quiet down there. Homer has some sheep, hasn't he?"

"Yes," said Mrs. Arable. "But it all started with that

pig we let Fern raise on a bottle. She calls him Wilbur. Homer bought the pig, and ever since it left our place Fern has been going to her uncle's to be near it."

"I've been hearing things about that pig," said Dr. Dorian, opening his eyes. "They say he's quite a pig."

"Have you heard about the words that appeared in the spider's web?" asked Mrs. Arable nervously.

"Yes," replied the doctor.

"Well, do you understand it?" asked Mrs. Arable.

"Understand what?"

"Do you understand how there could be any writing in a spider's web?"

"Oh, no," said Dr. Dorian. "I don't understand it.

But for that matter I don't understand how a spider learned to spin a web in the first place. When the words appeared, everyone said they were a miracle. But nobody pointed out that the web itself is a miracle."

"What's miraculous about a spider's web?" said Mrs.

Arable. "I don't see why you say a web is a miracle— it's just a web."

"Ever try to spin one?" asked Dr. Dorian.

Mrs. Arable shifted uneasily in her chair. "No," she replied. "But I can crochet a doily and I can knit a sock."

"Sure," said the doctor. "But somebody taught you, didn't they?"

"My mother taught me."

"Well, who taught a spider? A young spider knows how to spin a web without any instructions from anybody. Don't you regard that as a miracle?"

"I suppose so," said Mrs. Arable. "I never looked at it that way before. Still, I don't understand how those words got into the web. I don't understand it, and I don't like what I can't understand."

"None of us do," said Dr. Dorian, sighing. "I'm a doctor. Doctors are supposed to understand everything. But I don't understand everything, and I don't intend to let it worry me."

Mrs. Arable fidgeted. "Fern says the animals talk to each other. Dr. Dorian, do you believe animals talk?"

"I never heard one say anything," he replied. "But that proves nothing. It is quite possible that an animal has spoken civilly to me and that I didn't catch the remark because I wasn't paying attention. Children pay better attention than grownups. If Fern says that the animals in Zuckerman's barn talk, I'm quite ready to believe her. Perhaps if people talked less, animals would talk more. People are incessant talkers—I can give you my word on that."

"Well, I feel better about Fern," said Mrs. Arable. "You don't think I need worry about her?"

"Does she look well?" asked the doctor.

"Oh, yes."

"Appetite good?"

"Oh, yes, she's always hungry."

"Sleep well at night?"

"Oh, yes."

"Then don't worry," said the doctor.

"Do you think she'll ever start thinking about something besides pigs and sheep and geese and spiders?"

"How old is Fern?"

"She's eight."

"Well," said Dr. Dorian, "I think she will always love animals. But I doubt that she spends her entire life in Homer Zuckerman's barn cellar. How about boys—does she know any boys?"

"She knows Henry Fussy," said Mrs. Arable brightly.

Dr. Dorian closed his eyes again and went into deep thought. "Henry Fussy," he mumbled. "Hmm. Remarkable. Well, I don't think you have anything to worry about. Let Fern associate with her friends in the barn if she wants to. I would say, offhand, that spiders and pigs were fully as interesting as Henry Fussy. Yet I predict that the day will come when even Henry will drop some chance remark that catches Fern's attention. It's amazing how children change from year to year. How's Avery?" he asked, opening his eyes wide.

"Oh, Avery," chuckled Mrs. Arable. "Avery is always fine. Of course, he gets into poison ivy and gets stung by wasps and bees and brings frogs and snakes home and breaks everything he lays his hands on. He's fine."

"Good!" said the doctor.

Mrs. Arable said goodbye and thanked Dr. Dorian very much for his advice. She felt greatly relieved.

XV. *The Crickets*

THE CRICKETS sang in the grasses. They sang the song of summer's ending, a sad, monotonous song. "Summer is over and gone," they sang. "Over and gone, over and gone. Summer is dying, dying."

The crickets felt it was their duty to warn everybody that summertime cannot last forever. Even on the most beautiful days in the whole year—the days when summer is changing into fall—the crickets spread the rumor of sadness and change.

Everybody heard the song of the crickets. Avery and Fern Arable heard it as they walked the dusty road. They knew that school would soon begin again. The young geese heard it and knew that they would never be little goslings again. Charlotte heard it and knew that she hadn't much time left. Mrs. Zuckerman, at work in the kitchen, heard the crickets, and a sadness came over her, too. "Another summer gone," she sighed. Lurvy, at work building a crate for Wilbur, heard the song and knew it was time to dig potatoes.

"Summer is over and gone," repeated the crickets. "How many nights till frost?" sang the crickets. "Good-bye, summer, good-bye, good-bye!"

The sheep heard the crickets, and they felt so uneasy they broke a hole in the pasture fence and wandered up into the field across the road. The gander discovered the hole and led his family through, and they walked to the orchard and ate the apples that were lying on the ground. A little maple tree in the swamp heard the cricket song and turned bright red with anxiety.

Wilbur was now the center of attraction on the farm. Good food and regular hours were showing results: Wilbur was a pig any man would be proud of. One day more than a hundred people came to stand at his yard and admire him. Charlotte had written the word RA-DIANT, and Wilbur really looked radiant as he stood in the golden sunlight. Ever since the spider had befriended him, he had done his best to live up to his reputation. When Charlotte's web said SOME PIG, Wilbur had tried hard to look like some pig. When Charlotte's web said TERRIFIC, Wilbur had tried to look terrific. And now that the web said RADIANT, he did everything possible to make himself glow.

It is not easy to look radiant, but Wilbur threw himself into it with a will. He would turn his head slightly and blink his long eye-lashes. Then he would breathe deeply. And when his audience grew bored, he would spring into the air and do a back flip with a half twist. At this the crowd would yell and cheer. "How's that for a pig?" Mr. Zuckerman would ask, well pleased with himself. "That pig is radiant."

Some of Wilbur's friends in the barn worried for fear all this attention would go to his head and make him stuck up. But it never did. Wilbur was modest; fame did not spoil him. He still worried some about the future, as he could hardly believe that a mere spider would be able to save his life. Sometimes at night he would have a bad dream. He would dream that men were coming to get him with knives and guns. But that was only a dream. In the daytime, Wilbur usually felt happy and confident. No pig ever had truer friends, and he realized that friendship is one of the most satisfying things in the world. Even the song of the crickets did not make Wilbur too sad. He knew it was almost time for the County Fair, and he was looking forward to the trip. If he could distinguish himself at the Fair, and maybe win some prize money, he was sure Zuckerman would let him live.

Charlotte had worries of her own, but she kept quiet about them. One morning Wilbur asked her about the Fair.

"You're going *with* me, aren't you, Charlotte?" he said.

"Well, I don't know," replied Charlotte. "The Fair

comes at a bad time for me. I shall find it inconvenient to leave home, even for a few days."

"Why?" asked Wilbur.

"Oh, I just don't feel like leaving my web. Too much going on around here."

"*Please* come with me!" begged Wilbur. "I need you, Charlotte. I can't stand going to the Fair without you. You've just *got* to come."

"No," said Charlotte, "I believe I'd better stay home and see if I can't get some work done."

"What kind of work?" asked Wilbur.

"Egg laying. It's time I made an egg sac and filled it with eggs."

"I didn't know you could lay eggs," said Wilbur in amazement.

"Oh, sure," said the spider. "I'm versatile."

"What does 'versatile' mean—full of eggs?" asked Wilbur.

"Certainly not," said Charlotte. " 'Versatile' means I can turn with ease from one thing to another. It means I don't have to limit my activities to spinning and trapping and stunts like that."

"Why don't you come with me to the Fair Grounds and lay your eggs there?" pleaded Wilbur. "It would be wonderful fun."

Charlotte gave her web a twitch and moodily watched it sway. "I'm afraid not," she said. "You don't know the first thing about egg laying, Wilbur. I can't arrange my family duties to suit the management of the County Fair. When I get ready to lay eggs, I have to lay eggs, Fair or no Fair. However, I don't want you to worry about it—you might lose weight. We'll leave it this way: I'll come to the Fair if I possibly can."

"Oh, good!" said Wilbur. "I knew you wouldn't forsake me just when I need you most."

All that day Wilbur stayed inside, taking life easy in the straw. Charlotte rested and ate a grasshopper. She knew that she couldn't help Wilbur much longer. In a few days she would have to drop everything and build the beautiful little sac that would hold her eggs.

XVI. Off to the Fair

THE NIGHT before the County Fair, everybody went to bed early. Fern and Avery
were in bed by eight. Avery lay dreaming
that the Ferris wheel had stopped and that
he was in the top car. Fern lay dreaming that she was
getting sick in the swings.

Lurvy was in bed by eight-thirty. He lay dreaming
that he was throwing baseballs at a cloth cat and
winning a genuine Navajo blanket. Mr. and Mrs.
Zuckerman were in bed by nine. Mrs. Zuckerman lay
dreaming about a deep freeze unit. Mr. Zuckerman lay

dreaming about Wilbur. He dreamt that Wilbur had grown until he was one hundred and sixteen feet long and ninety-two feet high and that he had won all the prizes at the Fair and was covered with blue ribbons and even had a blue ribbon tied to the end of his tail.

Down in the barn cellar, the animals, too, went to sleep early, all except Charlotte. Tomorrow would be Fair Day. Every creature planned to get up early to see Wilbur off on his great adventure.

When morning came, everybody got up at daylight. The day was hot. Up the road at the Arables' house, Fern lugged a pail of hot water to her room and took a sponge bath. Then she put on her prettiest dress because she knew she would see boys at the Fair. Mrs. Arable scrubbed the back of Avery's neck, and wet his hair, and parted it, and brushed it down hard till it stuck to the top of his head—all but about six hairs that stood straight up. Avery put on clean underwear, clean blue jeans, and a clean shirt. Mr. Arable dressed, ate breakfast, and then went out and polished his truck. He had offered to drive everybody to the Fair, including Wilbur.

Bright and early, Lurvy put clean straw in Wilbur's crate and lifted it into the pigpen. The crate was green. In gold letters it said:

ZUCKERMAN'S FAMOUS PIG

Charlotte had her web looking fine for the occasion. Wilbur ate his breakfast slowly. He tried to look radiant without getting food in his ears.

In the kitchen, Mrs. Zuckerman suddenly made an announcement.

"Homer," she said to her husband, "I am going to give that pig a buttermilk bath."

"A what?" said Mr. Zuckerman.

"A buttermilk bath. My grandmother used to bathe her pig with buttermilk when it got dirty—I just remembered."

"Wilbur's not dirty," said Mr. Zuckerman proudly.

"He's filthy behind the ears," said Mrs. Zuckerman. "Every time Lurvy slops him, the food runs down around the ears. Then it dries and forms a crust. He also has a smudge on one side where he lays in the manure."

"He lays in clean straw," corrected Mr. Zuckerman.

"Well, he's dirty, and he's going to have a bath."

Mr. Zuckerman sat down weakly and ate a doughnut. His wife went to the woodshed. When she returned, she wore rubber boots and an old raincoat, and she carried a bucket of buttermilk and a small wooden paddle.

"Edith, you're crazy," mumbled Zuckerman.

But she paid no attention to him. Together they walked to the pigpen. Mrs. Zuckerman wasted no time. She climbed in with Wilbur and went to work. Dipping her paddle in the buttermilk, she rubbed him all over. The geese gathered around to see the fun, and so did the sheep and lambs. Even Templeton poked his head out cautiously, to watch Wilbur get a buttermilk bath. Charlotte got so interested, she lowered herself

on a dragline so she could see better. Wilbur stood still and closed his eyes. He could feel the buttermilk trickling down his sides. He opened his mouth and some buttermilk ran in. It was delicious. He felt radiant and happy. When Mrs. Zuckerman got through and rubbed him dry, he was the cleanest, prettiest pig you ever saw.

He was pure white, pink around the ears and snout, and smooth as silk.

The Zuckermans went up to change into their best clothes. Lurvy went to shave and put on his plaid shirt and his purple necktie. The animals were left to themselves in the barn.

The seven goslings paraded round and round their mother.

"Please, please, please take us to the Fair!" begged a gosling. Then all seven began teasing to go.

"Please, please, please, please, please, please . . ." They made quite a racket.

"Children!" snapped the goose. "We're staying quietly-ietly-ietly at home. Only Wilbur-ilbur-ilbur is going to the Fair."

Just then Charlotte interrupted.

"I shall go, too," she said, softly. "I have decided to go with Wilbur. He may need me. We can't tell what may happen at the Fair Grounds. Somebody's got to go along who knows how to write. And I think Templeton better come, too—I might need somebody to run errands and do general work."

"I'm staying right here," grumbled the rat. "I haven't the slightest interest in fairs."

"That's because you've never been to one," remarked the old sheep. "A fair is a rat's paradise. Everybody spills food at a fair. A rat can creep out late at night and have a feast. In the horse barn you will find oats that the trotters and pacers have spilled. In the trampled grass of the infield you will find old discarded lunch boxes containing the foul remains of peanut butter sandwiches, hard-boiled eggs, cracker crumbs, bits of doughnuts, and particles of cheese. In the hard-packed dirt of the midway, after the glaring lights are out and the people have gone home to bed, you will find a veritable treasure of popcorn fragments, frozen custard dribblings, candied apples abandoned by tired children, sugar fluff crystals, salted almonds, popsicles, partially gnawed ice cream cones, and the wooden sticks of lollypops. Everywhere is loot for a rat—in tents, in booths, in hay lofts—why, a fair has enough disgusting leftover food to satisfy a whole army of rats."

Templeton's eyes were blazing.

"Is this true?" he asked. "Is this appetizing yarn of yours true? I like high living, and what you say tempts me."

"It is true," said the old sheep. "Go to the Fair, Templeton. You will find that the conditions at a fair will surpass your wildest dreams. Buckets with sour mash sticking to them, tin cans containing particles of tuna fish, greasy paper bags stuffed with rotten . . ."

"That's enough!" cried Templeton. "Don't tell me any more. I'm going."

"Good," said Charlotte, winking at the old sheep.

"Now then—there is no time to be lost. Wilbur will soon be put into the crate. Templeton and I must get in the crate right now and hide ourselves."

The rat didn't waste a minute. He scampered over to the crate, crawled between the slats, and pulled straw up over him so he was hidden from sight.

"All right," said Charlotte, "I'm next." She sailed into the air, let out a dragline, and dropped gently to the ground. Then she climbed the side of the crate and hid herself inside a knothole in the top board.

The old sheep nodded. "What a cargo!" she said. "That sign ought to say 'Zuckerman's Famous Pig and Two Stowaways'."

"Look out, the people are coming-oming-oming!" shouted the gander. "Cheese it, cheese it, cheese it!"

The big truck with Mr. Arable at the wheel backed slowly down toward the barnyard. Lurvy and Mr. Zuckerman walked alongside. Fern and Avery were standing in the body of the truck hanging on to the sideboards.

"Listen to me," whispered the old sheep to Wilbur. "When they open the crate and try to put you in, struggle! Don't go without a tussle. Pigs always resist when they are being loaded."

"If I struggle I'll get dirty," said Wilbur.

"Never mind that—do as I say! Struggle! If you were to walk into the crate without resisting, Zuckerman might think you were bewitched. He'd be scared to go to the Fair."

Templeton poked his head up through the straw. "Struggle if you must," said he, "but kindly remember that I'm hiding down here in this crate and I don't want to be stepped on, or kicked in the face, or pummeled, or crushed in any way, or squashed, or buffeted about, or bruised, or lacerated, or scarred, or biffed. Just watch what you're doing, Mr. Radiant, when they get shoving you in!"

"Be quiet, Templeton!" said the sheep. "Pull in your head—they're coming. Look radiant, Wilbur! Lay low, Charlotte! Talk it up, geese!"

The truck backed slowly to the pigpen and stopped. Mr. Arable cut the motor, got out, walked around to the rear, and lowered the tailgate. The geese cheered. Mrs. Arable got out of the truck. Fern and Avery jumped to the ground. Mrs. Zuckerman came walking down from the house. Everybody lined up at the fence and stood for a moment admiring Wilbur and the beautiful green crate. Nobody realized that the crate already contained a rat and a spider.

"That's some pig!" said Mrs. Arable.

"He's terrific," said Lurvy.

"He's very radiant," said Fern, remembering the day he was born.

"Well," said Mrs. Zuckerman, "he's clean, anyway. The buttermilk certainly helped."

Mr. Arable studied Wilbur carefully. "Yes, he's a wonderful pig," he said. "It's hard to believe that he was the runt of the litter. You'll get some extra good ham and bacon, Homer, when it comes time to kill *that* pig."

Wilbur heard these words and his heart almost stopped. "I think I'm going to faint," he whispered to the old sheep, who was watching.

"Kneel down!" whispered the old sheep. "Let the blood rush to your head!"

Wilbur sank to his knees, all radiance gone. His eyes closed.

"Look!" screamed Fern. "He's fading away!"

"Hey, watch me!" yelled Avery, crawling on all fours into the crate. "I'm a pig! I'm a pig!"

Avery's foot touched Templeton under the straw. "What a mess!" thought the rat. "What fantastic creatures boys are! Why did I let myself in for this?"

The geese saw Avery in the crate and cheered.

"Avery, you get out of that crate this instant!" commanded his mother. "What do you think you are?"

"I'm a pig!" cried Avery, tossing handfuls of straw into the air. "Oink, oink, oink!"

"The truck is rolling away, Papa," said Fern.

The truck, with no one at the wheel, had started to

roll downhill. Mr. Arable dashed to the driver's seat and pulled on the emergency brake. The truck stopped. The geese cheered. Charlotte crouched and made herself as small as possible in the knothole, so Avery wouldn't see her.

"Come out at once!" cried Mrs. Arable. Avery crawled out of the crate on hands and knees, making faces at Wilbur. Wilbur fainted away.

"The pig has passed out," said Mrs. Zuckerman. "Throw water on him!"

"Throw buttermilk!" suggested Avery.

The geese cheered.

Lurvy ran for a pail of water. Fern climbed into the pen and knelt by Wilbur's side.

"It's sunstroke," said Zuckerman. "The heat is too much for him."

"Maybe he's dead," said Avery.

"Come out of that pigpen *immediately!*" cried Mrs. Arable. Avery obeyed his mother and climbed into the back of the truck so he could see better. Lurvy returned with cold water and dashed it on Wilbur.

"Throw some on me!" cried Avery. "I'm hot, too."

"Oh, keep quiet!" hollered Fern. "Keep *qui*-ut!" Her eyes were brimming with tears.

Wilbur, feeling the cold water, came to. He rose slowly to his feet, while the geese cheered.

"He's up!" said Mr. Arable. "I guess there's nothing wrong with him."

"I'm hungry," said Avery. "I want a candied apple."

"Wilbur's all right now," said Fern. "We can start. I want to take a ride in the Ferris wheel."

Mr. Zuckerman and Mr. Arable and Lurvy grabbed the pig and pushed him headfirst toward the crate. Wilbur began to struggle. The harder the men pushed, the harder he held back. Avery jumped down and joined the men. Wilbur kicked and thrashed and grunted. "Nothing wrong with *this* pig," said Mr. Zuckerman cheerfully, pressing his knee against Wilbur's behind. "All together, now, boys! Shove!"

With a final heave they jammed him into the crate. The geese cheered. Lurvy nailed some boards across the end, so Wilbur couldn't back out. Then, using all their strength, the men picked up the crate and heaved it aboard the truck. They did not know that under the straw was a rat, and inside a knothole was a big grey spider. They saw only a pig.

"Everybody in!" called Mr. Arable. He started the motor. The ladies climbed in beside him. Mr. Zuckerman and Lurvy and Fern and Avery rode in back, hanging onto the sideboards. The truck began to move ahead. The geese cheered. The children answered their cheer, and away went everybody to the Fair.

XVII. Uncle

WHEN they pulled into the Fair Grounds, they could hear music and see the Ferris wheel turning in the sky. They could smell the dust of the race track where the sprinkling cart had moistened it; and they could smell hamburgers frying and see balloons aloft. They could hear sheep blatting in their pens. An enormous voice over the loudspeaker said: "Attention, please! Will the owner of a Pontiac car, license number H-2439, please move your car away from the fireworks shed!"

"Can I have some money?" asked Fern.

"Can I, too?" asked Avery.

"I'm going to win a doll by spinning a wheel and it will stop at the right number," said Fern.

"I'm going to steer a jet plane and make it bump into another one."

"Can I have a balloon?" asked Fern.

"Can I have a frozen custard and a cheeseburger and some raspberry soda pop?" asked Avery.

"You children be quiet till we get the pig unloaded," said Mrs. Arable.

"Let's let the children go off by themselves," suggested Mr. Arable. "The Fair only comes once a year." Mr. Arable gave Fern two quarters and two dimes. He gave Avery five dimes and four nickels. "Now run along!" he said. "And remember, the money has to last *all day*. Don't spend it all the first few minutes. And be back here at the truck at noontime so we can all have lunch together. And don't eat a lot of stuff that's going to make you sick to your stomachs."

"And if you go in those swings," said Mrs. Arable, "you hang on tight! You hang on *very* tight. Hear me?"

"And don't get lost!" said Mrs. Zuckerman.

"And don't get dirty!"

"Don't get overheated!" said their mother.

"Watch out for pickpockets!" cautioned their father.

"And don't cross the race track when the horses are coming!" cried Mrs. Zuckerman.

The children grabbed each other by the hand and danced off in the direction of the merry-go-round, toward the wonderful music and the wonderful adventure and the wonderful excitement, into the wonderful midway where there would be no parents to guard them and guide them, and where they could be happy and free and do as they pleased. Mrs. Arable stood quietly

and watched them go. Then she sighed. Then she blew her nose.

"Do you really think it's all right?" she asked.

"Well, they've got to grow up some time," said Mr. Arable. "And a fair is a good place to start, I guess."

While Wilbur was being unloaded and taken out of his crate and into his new pigpen, crowds gathered to watch. They stared at the sign ZUCKERMAN'S FAMOUS PIG. Wilbur stared back and tried to look extra good. He was pleased with his new home. The pen was grassy, and it was shaded from the sun by a shed roof.

Charlotte, watching her chance, scrambled out of the crate and climbed a post to the under side of the roof. Nobody noticed her.

Templeton, not wishing to come out in broad daylight, stayed quietly under the straw at the bottom of the crate. Mr. Zuckerman poured some skim milk into Wilbur's trough, pitched clean straw into his pen, and then he and Mrs. Zuckerman and the Arables walked away toward the cattle barn to look at purebred cows and to see the sights. Mr. Zuckerman particularly wanted to look at tractors. Mrs. Zuckerman wanted to see a deep freeze. Lurvy wandered off by himself, hoping to meet friends and have some fun on the midway.

As soon as the people were gone, Charlotte spoke to Wilbur.

"It's a good thing you can't see what *I* see," she said.

"What do you see?" asked Wilbur.

"There's a pig in the next pen and he's enormous. I'm afraid he's much bigger than you are."

"Maybe he's older than I am, and has had more time to grow," suggested Wilbur. Tears began to come to his eyes.

"I'll drop down and have a closer look," Charlotte said. Then she crawled along a beam till she was directly over the next pen. She let herself down on a dragline until she hung in the air just in front of the big pig's snout.

"May I have your name?" she asked, politely.

The pig stared at her. "No name," he said in a big, hearty voice. "Just call me Uncle."

"Very well, Uncle," replied Charlotte. "What is the date of your birth? Are you a spring pig?"

"Sure I'm a spring pig," replied Uncle. "What did you think I was, a spring chicken? Haw, haw—that's a good one, eh, Sister?"

"Mildly funny," said Charlotte. "I've heard funnier ones, though. Glad to have met you, and now I must be going."

She ascended slowly and returned to Wilbur's pen.

"He claims he's a spring pig," reported Charlotte,

"and perhaps he is. One thing is certain, he has a most unattractive personality. He is too familiar, too noisy, and he cracks weak jokes. Also, he's not anywhere near as clean as you are, nor as pleasant. I took quite a dislike to him in our brief interview. He's going to be a hard pig to beat, though, Wilbur, on account of his size and weight. But with me helping you, it can be done."

"When are you going to spin a web?" asked Wilbur.

"This afternoon, late, if I'm not too tired," said

Charlotte. "The least thing tires me these days. I don't seem to have the energy I once had. My age, I guess."

Wilbur looked at his friend. She looked rather swollen and she seemed listless.

"I'm awfully sorry to hear that you're feeling poorly, Charlotte," he said. "Perhaps if you spin a web and catch a couple of flies you'll feel better."

"Perhaps," she said, wearily. "But I feel like the end of a long day." Clinging upside down to the ceiling, she settled down for a nap, leaving Wilbur very much worried.

All morning people wandered past Wilbur's pen. Dozens and dozens of strangers stopped to stare at him and to admire his silky white coat, his curly tail, his kind and radiant expression. Then they would move on to the next pen where the bigger pig lay. Wilbur heard several people make favorable remarks about Uncle's great size. He couldn't help overhearing these remarks, and he couldn't help worrying. "And now, with Charlotte not feeling well . . ." he thought. "Oh, dear!"

All morning Templeton slept quietly under the straw. The day grew fiercely hot. At noon the Zuckermans and the Arables returned to the pigpen. Then, a few minutes later, Fern and Avery showed up. Fern had a monkey doll in her arms and was eating Crackerjack. Avery had a balloon tied to his ear and was chewing a candied apple. The children were hot and dirty.

"Isn't it hot?" said Mrs. Zuckerman.

"It's *terribly* hot," said Mrs. Arable, fanning herself with an advertisement of a deep freeze.

One by one they climbed into the truck and opened lunch boxes. The sun beat down on everything. Nobody seemed hungry.

"When are the judges going to decide about Wilbur?" asked Mrs. Zuckerman.

"Not till tomorrow," said Mr. Zuckerman.

Lurvy appeared, carrying an Indian blanket that he had won.

"That's just what we need," said Avery. "A blanket."

"Of course it is," replied Lurvy. And he spread the blanket across the sideboards of the truck so that it was like a little tent. The children sat in the shade, under the blanket, and felt better.

After lunch, they stretched out and fell asleep.

XVIII. The Cool of the Evening

IN THE cool of the evening, when shadows darkened the Fair Grounds, Templeton crept from the crate and looked around. Wilbur lay asleep in the straw. Charlotte was building a web. Templeton's keen nose detected many fine smells in the air. The rat was hungry and thirsty. He decided to go exploring. Without saying anything to anybody, he started off.

"Bring me back a word!" Charlotte called after him. "I shall be writing tonight for the last time."

The rat mumbled something to himself and disappeared into the shadows. He did not like being treated like a messenger boy.

After the heat of the day, the evening came as a welcome relief to all. The Ferris wheel was lighted now. It went round and round in the sky and seemed twice as high as by day. There were lights on the midway, and you could hear the crackle of the gambling machines and the music of the merry-go-round and the voice of the man in the beano booth calling numbers.

The children felt refreshed after their nap. Fern met

her friend Henry Fussy, and he invited her to ride with him in the Ferris wheel. He even bought a ticket for her, so it didn't cost her anything. When Mrs. Arable happened to look up into the starry sky and saw her little daughter sitting with Henry Fussy and going higher and higher into the air, and saw how happy Fern looked, she just shook her head. "My, my!" she said. "Henry Fussy. Think of that!"

Templeton kept out of sight. In the tall grass behind the cattle barn he found a folded newspaper. Inside it were leftovers from somebody's lunch: a deviled ham sandwich, a piece of Swiss cheese, part of a hard-boiled egg, and the core of a wormy apple. The rat crawled in and ate everything. Then he tore a word out of the paper, rolled it up, and started back to Wilbur's pen.

Charlotte had her web almost finished when Templeton returned, carrying the newspaper clipping. She had left a space in the middle of the web. At this hour, no people were around the pigpen, so the rat and the spider and the pig were by themselves.

"I hope you brought a good one," Charlotte said. "It is the last word I shall ever write."

"Here," said Templeton, unrolling the paper.

"What does it say?" asked Charlotte. "You'll have to read it for me."

"It says 'Humble,' " replied the rat.

"Humble?" said Charlotte. " 'Humble' has two meanings. It means 'not proud' and it means 'near the ground.' That's Wilbur all over. He's not proud and he's near the ground."

"Well, I hope you're satisfied," sneered the rat. "I'm not going to spend all my time fetching and carrying. I came to this Fair to enjoy myself, not to deliver papers."

"You've been very helpful," Charlotte said. "Run along, if you want to see more of the Fair."

The rat grinned. "I'm going to make a night of it," he said. "The old sheep was right—this Fair is a rat's paradise. What eating! And what drinking! And everywhere good hiding and good hunting. Bye, bye, my humble Wilbur! Fare thee well, Charlotte, you old schemer! This will be a night to remember in a rat's life."

He vanished into the shadows.

Charlotte went back to her work. It was quite dark now. In the distance, fireworks began going off—rockets, scattering fiery balls in the sky. By the time the

Arables and the Zuckermans and Lurvy returned from the grandstand, Charlotte had finished her web. The word HUMBLE was woven neatly in the center. Nobody noticed it in the darkness. Everyone was tired and happy.

Fern and Avery climbed into the truck and lay down. They pulled the Indian blanket over them. Lurvy gave Wilbur a forkful of fresh straw. Mr. Arable patted him. "Time for us to go home," he said to the pig. "See you tomorrow."

The grownups climbed slowly into the truck and Wilbur heard the engine start and then heard the truck moving away in low speed. He would have felt lonely and homesick, had Charlotte not been with him. He never felt lonely when she was near. In the distance he could still hear the music of the merry-go-round.

As he was dropping off to sleep he spoke to Charlotte.

"Sing me that song again, about the dung and the dark," he begged.

"Not tonight," she said in a low voice. "I'm too tired." Her voice didn't seem to come from her web.

"Where are you?" asked Wilbur. "I can't see you. Are you on your web?"

"I'm back here," she answered. "Up in this back corner."

"Why aren't you on your web?" asked Wilbur. "You almost *never* leave your web."

"I've left it tonight," she said.

Wilbur closed his eyes. "Charlotte," he said, after a while, "do you really think Zuckerman will let me live and not kill me when the cold weather comes? Do you really think so?"

"Of course," said Charlotte. "You are a famous pig and you are a good pig. Tomorrow you will probably win a prize. The whole world will hear about you. Zuckerman will be proud and happy to own such a pig. You have nothing to fear, Wilbur—nothing to worry about. Maybe you'll live forever—who knows? And now, go to sleep."

For a while there was no sound. Then Wilbur's voice:

"What are you doing up there, Charlotte?"

"Oh, making something," she said. "Making something, as usual."

"Is it something for me?" asked Wilbur.

"No," said Charlotte. "It's something for *me*, for a change."

"Please tell me what it is," begged Wilbur.

"I'll tell you in the morning," she said. "When the first light comes into the sky and the sparrows stir and the cows rattle their chains, when the rooster crows and the stars fade, when early cars whisper along the highway, you look up here and I'll show you something. I will show you my masterpiece."

Before she finished the sentence, Wilbur was asleep. She could tell by the sound of his breathing that he was sleeping peacefully, deep in the straw.

Miles away, at the Arables' house, the men sat around the kitchen table eating a dish of canned peaches and talking over the events of the day. Upstairs, Avery was already in bed and asleep. Mrs. Arable was tucking Fern into bed.

"Did you have a good time at the Fair?" she asked as she kissed her daughter.

Fern nodded. "I had the best time I have ever had anywhere or any time in all of my whole life."

"Well!" said Mrs. Arable. "Isn't that nice!"

XIX. *The Egg Sac*

NEXT morning when the first light came into the sky and the sparrows stirred in the trees, when the cows rattled their chains and the rooster crowed and the early automobiles went whispering along the road, Wilbur awoke and looked for Charlotte. He saw her up overhead in a corner near the back of his pen. She was very quiet. Her eight legs were spread wide. She seemed to have shrunk during the night. Next to her, attached to the ceiling, Wilbur saw a curious object. It was a sort of sac, or cocoon. It was peach-colored and looked as though it were made of cotton candy.

"Are you awake, Charlotte?" he said softly.

"Yes," came the answer.

"What is that nifty little thing? Did you make it?"

"I did indeed," replied Charlotte in a weak voice.

"Is it a plaything?"

"Plaything? I should say not. It is my egg sac, my *magnum opus*."

"I don't know what a magnum opus is," said Wilbur.

"That's Latin," explained Charlotte. "It means 'great work.' This egg sac is my great work—the finest thing I have ever made."

"What's inside it?" asked Wilbur. "Eggs?"

"Five hundred and fourteen of them," she replied.

"Five *hundred* and four*teen*?" said Wilbur. "You're kidding."

"No, I'm not. I counted them. I got started counting, so I kept on—just to keep my mind occupied."

"It's a perfectly beautiful egg sac," said Wilbur, feeling as happy as though he had constructed it himself.

"Yes, it *is* pretty," replied Charlotte, patting the sac with her two front legs. "Anyway, I can guarantee that it is strong. It's made out of the toughest material I have. It is also waterproof. The eggs are inside and will be warm and dry."

"Charlotte," said Wilbur dreamily, "are you really going to have five hundred and fourteen children?"

"If nothing happens, yes," she said. "Of course, they won't show up till next spring." Wilbur noticed that Charlotte's voice sounded sad.

"What makes you sound so down-hearted? I should think you'd be terribly happy about this."

"Oh, don't pay any attention to me," said Charlotte. "I just don't have much pep any more. I guess I feel sad because I won't ever see my children."

"What do you mean you won't see your children! Of *course* you will. We'll *all* see them. It's going to be simply wonderful next spring in the barn cellar with five hundred and fourteen baby spiders running around all over the place. And the geese will have a new set of goslings, and the sheep will have their new lambs . . ."

"Maybe," said Charlotte quietly. "However, I have a feeling I'm not going to see the results of last night's efforts. I don't feel good at all. I think I'm languishing, to tell you the truth."

Wilbur didn't understand the word "languish" and he hated to bother Charlotte by asking her to explain. But he was so worried he felt he had to ask.

"What does 'languishing' mean?"

"It means I'm slowing up, feeling my age. I'm not young any more, Wilbur. But I don't want you to worry about me. This is your big day today. Look at my web—doesn't it show up well with the dew on it?"

Charlotte's web never looked more beautiful than it looked this morning. Each strand held dozens of bright drops of early morning dew. The light from the east struck it and made it all plain and clear. It was a perfect piece of designing and building. In another hour or two, a steady stream of people would pass by, admiring it, and reading it, and looking at Wilbur, and marveling at the miracle.

As Wilbur was studying the web, a pair of whiskers and a sharp face appeared. Slowly Templeton dragged himself across the pen and threw himself down in a corner.

"I'm back," he said in a husky voice. "What a night!"

The rat was swollen to twice his normal size. His stomach was as big around as a jelly jar.

"What a night!" he repeated, hoarsely. "What feasting and carousing! A real gorge! I must have eaten the remains of thirty lunches. Never have I seen such leavings, and everything well-ripened and seasoned with the passage of time and the heat of the day. Oh, it was rich, my friends, rich!"

"You ought to be ashamed of yourself," said Charlotte in disgust. "It would serve you right if you had an acute attack of indigestion."

"Don't worry about my stomach," snarled Templeton. "It can handle anything. And by the way, I've got some bad news. As I came past that pig next door—the one that calls himself Uncle—I noticed a blue tag on the front of his pen. That means he has won first prize. I guess you're licked, Wilbur. You might as well relax —nobody is going to hang any medal on *you*. Furthermore, I wouldn't be surprised if Zuckerman changes his mind about you. Wait till he gets hankering for some fresh pork and smoked ham and crisp bacon! He'll take the knife to you, my boy."

"Be still, Templeton!" said Charlotte. "You're too stuffed and bloated to know what you're saying. Don't pay any attention to him, Wilbur!"

Wilbur tried not to think about what the rat had just said. He decided to change the subject.

"Templeton," said Wilbur, "if you weren't so dopey, you would have noticed that Charlotte has made an egg sac. She is going to become a mother. For your information, there are five hundred and fourteen eggs in that peachy little sac."

"Is this true?" asked the rat, eyeing the sac suspiciously.

"Yes, it's true," sighed Charlotte.

"Congratulations!" murmured Templeton. "This *has* been a night!" He closed his eyes, pulled some straw over himself, and dropped off into a deep sleep. Wilbur and Charlotte were glad to be rid of him for a while.

At nine o'clock, Mr. Arable's truck rolled into the Fair Grounds and came to a stop at Wilbur's pen. Everybody climbed out.

"Look!" cried Fern. "Look at Charlotte's web! Look what it says!"

The grownups and the children joined hands and stood there, studying the new sign.

" 'Humble,' " said Mr. Zuckerman. "Now isn't that just the word for Wilbur!"

Everyone rejoiced to find that the miracle of the web had been repeated. Wilbur gazed up lovingly into their faces. He looked very humble and very grateful. Fern winked at Charlotte. Lurvy soon got busy. He poured a bucket of warm slops into the trough, and while Wilbur ate his breakfast Lurvy scratched him gently with a smooth stick.

"Wait a minute!" cried Avery. "Look at this!" He pointed to the blue tag on Uncle's pen. "This pig has won first prize already."

The Zuckermans and the Arables stared at the tag. Mrs. Zuckerman began to cry. Nobody said a word. They just stared at the tag. Then they stared at Uncle. Then they stared at the tag again. Lurvy took out an enormous handkerchief and blew his nose very loud— so loud, in fact, that the noise was heard by stableboys over at the horse barn.

"Can I have some money?" asked Fern. "I want to go out on the midway."

"You stay right where you are!" said her mother. Tears came to Fern's eyes.

"What's everybody crying about?" asked Mr. Zuckerman. "Let's get busy! Edith, bring the buttermilk!"

Mrs. Zuckerman wiped her eyes with her handkerchief. She went to the truck and came back with a gallon jar of buttermilk.

"Bath time!" said Zuckerman, cheerfully. He and Mrs. Zuckerman and Avery climbed into Wilbur's pen. Avery slowly poured buttermilk on Wilbur's head and back, and as it trickled down his sides and cheeks, Mr. and Mrs. Zuckerman rubbed it into his hair and skin. Passersby stopped to watch. Pretty soon quite a crowd had gathered. Wilbur grew beautifully white and smooth. The morning sun shone through his pink ears.

"He isn't as big as that pig next door," remarked one bystander, "but he's cleaner. That's what I like."

"So do I," said another man.

"He's humble, too," said a woman, reading the sign on the web.

Everybody who visited the pigpen had a good word to say about Wilbur. Everyone admired the web. And of course nobody noticed Charlotte.

Suddenly a voice was heard on the loud speaker.

"Attention, please!" it said. "Will Mr. Homer Zuckerman bring his famous pig to the judges' booth in front of the grandstand. A special award will be made there in twenty minutes. Everyone is invited to attend. Crate your pig, please, Mr. Zuckerman, and report to the judges' booth promptly!"

For a moment after this announcement, the Arables and the Zuckermans were unable to speak or move. Then Avery picked up a handful of straw and threw it high in the air and gave a loud yell. The straw fluttered down like confetti into Fern's hair. Mr. Zuckerman hugged Mrs. Zuckerman. Mr. Arable kissed Mrs. Arable. Avery kissed Wilbur. Lurvy shook hands with everybody. Fern hugged her mother. Avery hugged Fern. Mrs. Arable hugged Mrs. Zuckerman.

Up overhead, in the shadows of the ceiling, Char-

lotte crouched unseen, her front legs encircling her egg sac. Her heart was not beating as strongly as usual and she felt weary and old, but she was sure at last that she had saved Wilbur's life, and she felt peaceful and contented.

"We have no time to lose!" shouted Mr. Zuckerman. "Lurvy, help with the crate!"

"Can I have some money?" asked Fern.

"You *wait!*" said Mrs. Arable. "Can't you see everybody is busy?"

"Put that empty buttermilk jar into the truck!" commanded Mr. Arable. Avery grabbed the jar and rushed to the truck.

"Does my hair look all right?" asked Mrs. Zuckerman.

"Looks fine," snapped Mr. Zuckerman, as he and Lurvy set the crate down in front of Wilbur.

"You didn't even *look* at my hair!" said Mrs. Zuckerman.

"You're all right, Edith," said Mrs. Arable. "Just keep calm."

Templeton, asleep in the straw, heard the commotion and awoke. He didn't know exactly what was going on, but when he saw the men shoving Wilbur into the crate he made up his mind to go along. He watched his chance and when no one was looking he crept into the crate and buried himself in the straw at the bottom.

"All ready, boys!" cried Mr. Zuckerman. "Let's go!" He and Mr. Arable and Lurvy and Avery grabbed the crate and boosted it over the side of the pen and up into the truck. Fern jumped aboard and sat on top of the crate. She still had straw in her hair and looked very pretty and excited. Mr. Arable started the motor. Everyone climbed in, and off they drove to the judge's booth in front of the grandstand.

As they passed the Ferris wheel, Fern gazed up at it and wished she were in the topmost car with Henry Fussy at her side.

XX. *The Hour of Triumph*

S PECIAL announcement!" said the loud speaker in a pompous voice. "The management of the Fair takes great pleasure in presenting Mr. Homer L. Zuckerman and his famous pig. The truck bearing this extraordinary animal is now approaching the infield. Kindly stand back and give the truck room to proceed! In a few moments the pig will be unloaded in the special judging ring in front of the grandstand, where a special award will be made. Will the crowd please make way and let the truck pass. Thank you."

Wilbur trembled when he heard this speech. He felt happy but dizzy. The truck crept along slowly in low speed. Crowds of people surrounded it, and Mr. Arable had to drive very carefully in order not to run over anybody. At last he managed to reach the judges' stand. Avery jumped out and lowered the tailgate.

"I'm scared to death," whispered Mrs. Zuckerman. "Hundreds of people are looking at us."

"Cheer up," replied Mrs. Arable, "this is fun."

"Unload your pig, please!" said the loud speaker.

"All together, now, boys!" said Mr. Zuckerman. Several men stepped forward from the crowd to help lift the crate. Avery was the busiest helper of all.

"Tuck your shirt in, Avery!" cried Mrs. Zuckerman. "And tighten your belt. Your pants are coming down."

"Can't you see I'm busy?" replied Avery in disgust.

"Look!" cried Fern, pointing. "There's Henry!"

"Don't shout, Fern!" said her mother. "And don't point!"

"Can't I *please* have some money?" asked Fern. "Henry invited me to go on the Ferris wheel again, only I don't think he has any money left. He ran out of money."

Mrs. Arable opened her handbag. "Here," she said. "Here is forty cents. Now don't get lost! And be back at our regular meeting place by the pigpen very soon!"

Fern raced off, ducking and dodging through the crowd, in search of Henry.

"The Zuckerman pig is now being taken from his crate," boomed the voice of the loud speaker. "Stand by for an announcement!"

Templeton crouched under the straw at the bottom of the crate. "What a lot of nonsense!" muttered the rat. "What a lot of fuss about nothing!"

Over in the pigpen, silent and alone, Charlotte rested. Her two front legs embraced the egg sac. Charlotte could hear everything that was said on the loud speaker. The words gave her courage. This was her hour of triumph.

As Wilbur came out of the crate, the crowd clapped and cheered. Mr. Zuckerman took off his cap and bowed. Lurvy pulled his big handkerchief from his pocket and wiped the sweat from the back of his neck. Avery knelt in the dirt by Wilbur's side, busily stroking him and showing off. Mrs. Zuckerman and Mrs. Arable stood on the running board of the truck.

"Ladeez and gentlemen," said the loud speaker, "we now present Mr. Homer L. Zuckerman's distinguished pig. The fame of this unique animal has spread to the far corners of the earth, attracting many valuable tourists to our great State. Many of you will recall that never-to-be-forgotten day last summer when the writing appeared mysteriously on the spider's web in Mr. Zuckerman's barn, calling the attention of all and sundry to the fact that this pig was completely out of the ordinary. This miracle has never been fully explained, although learned men have visited the Zuckerman pigpen to study and observe the phenomenon. In the last analysis, we simply know that we are dealing with supernatural forces here, and we should all feel proud and grateful. In the words of the spider's web, ladies and gentlemen, this is some pig."

Wilbur blushed. He stood perfectly still and tried to look his best.

"This magnificent animal," continued the loud speaker, "is truly terrific. Look at him, ladies and gentlemen! Note the smoothness and whiteness of the coat, observe the spotless skin, the healthy pink glow of ears and snout."

"It's the buttermilk," whispered Mrs. Arable to Mrs. Zuckerman.

"Note the general radiance of this animal! Then re-member the day when the word 'radiant' appeared clearly on the web. Whence came this mysterious writing? Not from the spider, we can rest assured of that. Spiders are very clever at weaving their webs, but needless to say spiders cannot write."

"Oh, they can't, can't they?" murmured Charlotte to herself.

"Ladeez and gentlemen," continued the loud speaker, "I must not take any more of your valuable time. On behalf of the governors of the Fair, I have the honor of awarding a special prize of twenty-five dollars to Mr. Zuckerman, together with a handsome bronze medal suitably engraved, in token of our appreciation of the part played by this pig—this radiant, this terrific, this humble pig—in attracting so many visitors to our great County Fair."

Wilbur had been feeling dizzier and dizzier through

this long, complimentary speech. When he heard the crowd begin to cheer and clap again, he suddenly fainted away. His legs collapsed, his mind went blank, and he fell to the ground, unconscious.

"What's wrong?" asked the loud speaker. "What's going on, Zuckerman? What's the trouble with your pig?"

Avery was kneeling by Wilbur's head, stroking him. Mr. Zuckerman was dancing about, fanning him with his cap.

"He's all right," cried Mr. Zuckerman. "He gets these spells. He's modest and can't stand praise."

"Well, we can't give a prize to a *dead* pig," said the loud speaker. "It's never been done."

"He isn't dead," hollered Zuckerman. "He's fainted. He gets embarrassed easily. Run for some water, Lurvy!"

Lurvy sprang from the judges' ring and disappeared.

Templeton poked his head from the straw. He noticed that the end of Wilbur's tail was within reach. Templeton grinned. "I'll tend to this," he chuckled. He took Wilbur's tail in his mouth and bit it, just as hard as he could bite. The pain revived Wilbur. In a flash he was back on his feet.

"Ouch!" he screamed.

"Hooray!" yelled the crowd. "He's up! The pig's up! Good work, Zuckerman! That's some pig!" Everyone was delighted. Mr. Zuckerman was the most pleased of all. He sighed with relief. Nobody had seen Templeton. The rat had done his work well.

And now one of the judges climbed into the ring with the prizes. He handed Mr. Zuckerman two ten dollar bills and a five dollar bill. Then he tied the medal around Wilbur's neck. Then he shook hands with Mr. Zuckerman while Wilbur blushed. Avery put out his hand and the judge shook hands with him, too. The crowd cheered. A photographer took Wilbur's picture.

A great feeling of happiness swept over the Zuckermans and the Arables. This was the greatest moment in Mr. Zuckerman's life. It is deeply satisfying to win a prize in front of a lot of people.

As Wilbur was being shoved back into the crate, Lurvy came charging through the crowd carrying a pail of water. His eyes had a wild look. Without hesitating a second, he dashed the water at Wilbur. In his excitement he missed his aim, and the water splashed all over Mr. Zuckerman and Avery. They got soaking wet.

"For goodness' sake!" bellowed Mr. Zuckerman, who was really drenched. "What ails you, Lurvy? Can't you see the pig is all right?"

"You asked for water," said Lurvy meekly.

"I didn't ask for a shower bath," said Mr. Zuckerman. The crowd roared with laughter. Finally Mr. Zuckerman had to laugh, too. And of course Avery was tickled to find himself so wet, and he immediately started to act like a clown. He pretended he was taking a shower bath; he made faces and danced around and rubbed imaginary soap under his armpits. Then he dried himself with an imaginary towel.

"Avery, stop it!" cried his mother. "Stop showing off!"

But the crowd loved it. Avery heard nothing but the applause. He liked being a clown in a ring, with everybody watching, in front of a grandstand. When he discovered there was still a little water left in the bottom of the pail, he raised the pail high in the air and dumped the water on himself and made faces. The children in the grandstand screamed with appreciation.

At last things calmed down. Wilbur was loaded into the truck. Avery was led from the ring by his mother and placed on the seat of the truck to dry off. The truck, driven by Mr. Arable, crawled slowly back to the pigpen. Avery's wet trousers made a big wet spot on the seat.

XXI. *Last Day*

CHARLOTTE and Wilbur were alone. The families had gone to look for Fern. Templeton was asleep. Wilbur lay resting after the excitement and strain of the ceremony. His medal still hung from his neck; by looking out of the corner of his eye he could see it.

"Charlotte," said Wilbur after a while, "why are you so quiet?"

"I like to sit still," she said. "I've always been rather quiet."

"Yes, but you seem specially so today. Do you feel all right?"

"A little tired, perhaps. But I feel peaceful. Your success in the ring this morning was, to a small degree, *my* success. Your future is assured. You will live, secure and safe, Wilbur. Nothing can harm you now. These autumn days will shorten and grow cold. The leaves will shake loose from the trees and fall. Christmas will come, then the snows of winter. You will live to enjoy the beauty of the frozen world, for you mean a great deal to Zuckerman and he will not harm you, ever. Winter will pass, the days will lengthen, the ice will melt in the pasture pond. The song sparrow will return and sing, the frogs will awake, the warm wind will blow again. All these sights and sounds and smells will be yours to enjoy, Wilbur—this lovely world, these precious days . . ."

Charlotte stopped. A moment later a tear came to Wilbur's eye. "Oh, Charlotte," he said. "To think that when I first met you I thought you were cruel and bloodthirsty!"

When he recovered from his emotion, he spoke again.

"Why did you do all this for me?" he asked. "I don't deserve it. I've never done anything for you."

"You have been my friend," replied Charlotte. "That in itself is a tremendous thing. I wove my webs for you because I liked you. After all, what's a life, anyway? We're born, we live a little while, we die. A spider's life can't help being something of a mess, with all this trapping and eating flies. By helping you, perhaps I was trying to lift up my life a trifle. Heaven knows anyone's life can stand a little of that."

"Well," said Wilbur. "I'm no good at making speeches. I haven't got your gift for words. But you have saved me, Charlotte, and I would gladly give my life for you—I really would."

"I'm sure you would. And I thank you for your generous sentiments."

"Charlotte," said Wilbur. "We're all going home today. The Fair is almost over. Won't it be wonderful to be back home in the barn cellar again with the sheep and the geese? Aren't you anxious to get home?"

For a moment Charlotte said nothing. Then she spoke in a voice so low Wilbur could hardly hear the words.

"I will not be going back to the barn," she said.

Wilbur leapt to his feet. "Not going back?" he cried. "Charlotte, what are you talking about?"

"I'm done for," she replied. "In a day or two I'll be dead. I haven't even strength enough to climb down into the crate. I doubt if I have enough silk in my spinnerets to lower me to the ground."

Hearing this, Wilbur threw himself down in an agony of pain and sorrow. Great sobs racked his body. He heaved and grunted with desolation. "Charlotte," he moaned. "Charlotte! My true friend!"

"Come now, let's not make a scene," said the spider. "Be quiet, Wilbur. Stop thrashing about!"

"But I can't *stand* it," shouted Wilbur. "I won't leave you here alone to die. If you're going to stay here I shall stay, too."

"Don't be ridiculous," said Charlotte. "You can't stay here. Zuckerman and Lurvy and John Arable and the others will be back any minute now, and they'll shove you into that crate and away you'll go. Besides, it wouldn't make any sense for you to stay. There would be no one to feed you. The Fair Grounds will soon be empty and deserted."

Wilbur was in a panic. He raced round and round the pen. Suddenly he had an idea—he thought of the egg sac and the five hundred and fourteen little spiders that would hatch in the spring. If Charlotte herself was unable to go home to the barn, at least he must take her children along.

Wilbur rushed to the front of his pen. He put his front feet up on the top board and gazed around. In the distance he saw the Arables and the Zuckermans approaching. He knew he would have to act quickly.

"Where's Templeton?" he demanded.

"He's in that corner, under the straw, asleep," said Charlotte.

Wilbur rushed over, pushed his strong snout under the rat, and tossed him into the air.

"Templeton!" screamed Wilbur. "Pay attention!"

The rat, surprised out of a sound sleep, looked first dazed then disgusted.

"What kind of monkeyshine is this?" he growled. "Can't a rat catch a wink of sleep without being rudely popped into the air?"

"Listen to me!" cried Wilbur. "Charlotte is very ill.

She has only a short time to live. She cannot accompany us home, because of her condition. Therefore, it is absolutely necessary that I take her egg sac with me. I can't reach it, and I can't climb. You are the only one that can get it. There's not a second to be lost. The people are coming—they'll be here in no time. Please, please, *please*, Templeton, climb up and get the egg sac."

The rat yawned. He straightened his whiskers. Then he looked up at the egg sac.

"So!" he said, in disgust. "So it's old Templeton to the rescue again, is it? Templeton do this, Templeton do that, Templeton please run down to the dump and get me a magazine clipping, Templeton please lend me a piece of string so I can spin a web."

"Oh, hurry!" said Wilbur. "Hurry up, Templeton!"

But the rat was in no hurry. He began imitating Wilbur's voice.

"So it's 'Hurry up, Templeton,' is it?" he said. "Ho, ho. And what thanks do I ever get for these services, I would like to know? Never a kind word for old Templeton, only abuse and wisecracks and side remarks. Never a kind word for a rat."

"Templeton," said Wilbur in desperation, "if you don't stop talking and get busy, all will be lost, and I will die of a broken heart. Please climb up!"

Templeton lay back in the straw. Lazily he placed

his forepaws behind his head and crossed his knees, in an attitude of complete relaxation.

"Die of a broken heart," he mimicked. "How touching! My, my! I notice that it's always me you come to when in trouble. But I've never heard of anyone's heart breaking on *my* account. Oh, no. Who cares anything about old Templeton?"

"Get up!" screamed Wilbur. "Stop acting like a spoiled child!"

Templeton grinned and lay still. "Who made trip after trip to the dump?" he asked. "Why, it was old Templeton! Who saved Charlotte's life by scaring that Arable boy away with a rotten goose egg? Bless my soul, I believe it was old Templeton. Who bit your tail and got you back on your feet this morning after you had fainted in front of the crowd? Old Templeton. Has it ever occurred to you that I'm sick of running errands and doing favors? What do you think I am, anyway, a rat-of-all-work?"

Wilbur was desperate. The people were coming. And the rat was failing him. Suddenly he remembered Templeton's fondness for food.

"Templeton," he said, "I will make you a solemn promise. Get Charlotte's egg sac for me, and from now on I will let you eat first, when Lurvy slops me. I will let you have your choice of everything in the trough and I won't touch a thing until you're through."

The rat sat up. "You mean that?" he said.

"I promise. I cross my heart."

"All right, it's a deal," said the rat. He walked to the wall and started to climb. His stomach was still swollen from last night's gorge. Groaning and com-

plaining, he pulled himself slowly to the ceiling. He crept along till he reached the egg sac. Charlotte moved aside for him. She was dying, but she still had strength enough to move a little. Then Templeton bared his long ugly teeth and began snipping the threads that fastened the sac to the ceiling. Wilbur watched from below.

"Use extreme care!" he said. "I don't want a single one of those eggs harmed."

"Thith thtuff thticks in my mouth," complained the rat. "It'th worth than caramel candy."

But Templeton worked away at the job, and managed to cut the sac adrift and carry it to the ground, where he dropped it in front of Wilbur. Wilbur heaved a great sigh of relief.

"Thank you, Templeton," he said. "I will never forget this as long as I live."

"Neither will I," said the rat, picking his teeth. "I feel as though I'd eaten a spool of thread. Well, home we go!"

Templeton crept into the crate and buried himself in the straw. He got out of sight just in time. Lurvy and John Arable and Mr. Zuckerman came along at that moment, followed by Mrs. Arable and Mrs. Zuckerman and Avery and Fern. Wilbur had already decided how he would carry the egg sac—there was only one way possible. He carefully took the little bundle in his mouth and held it there on top of his tongue. He remembered what Charlotte had told him—that the sac was waterproof and strong. It felt funny on his tongue and made him drool a bit. And of course he couldn't say anything. But as he was being shoved into the crate, he looked up at Charlotte and gave her a wink. She knew he was saying good-bye in the only way he could. And she knew her children were safe.

"Good-bye!" she whispered. Then she summoned all her strength and waved one of her front legs at him.

She never moved again. Next day, as the Ferris wheel was being taken apart and the race horses were being loaded into vans and the entertainers were packing up their belongings and driving away in their trailers, Charlotte died. The Fair Grounds were soon deserted. The sheds and buildings were empty and forlorn. The infield was littered with bottles and trash. Nobody, of the hundreds of people that had visited the Fair, knew that a grey spider had played the most important part of all. No one was with her when she died.

XXII. A Warm Wind

AND SO Wilbur came home to his beloved manure pile in the barn cellar. His was a strange homecoming. Around his neck he wore a medal of honor; in his mouth he held a sac of spider's eggs. There is no place like home, Wilbur thought, as he placed Charlotte's five hundred and fourteen unborn children carefully in a safe corner. The barn smelled good. His friends the sheep and the geese were glad to see him back.

The geese gave him a noisy welcome.

"Congratu-congratu-congratulations!" they cried. "Nice work."

Mr. Zuckerman took the medal from Wilbur's neck and hung it on a nail over the pigpen, where visitors could examine it. Wilbur himself could look at it whenever he wanted to.

In the days that followed, he was very happy. He grew to a great size. He no longer worried about being killed, for he knew that Mr. Zuckerman would keep him as long as he lived. Wilbur often thought of Charlotte. A few strands of her old web still hung in the doorway. Every day Wilbur would stand and look at the torn, empty web, and a lump would come to his throat. No one had ever had such a friend—so affectionate, so loyal, and so skillful.

The autumn days grew shorter, Lurvy brought the squashes and pumpkins in from the garden and piled them on the barn floor, where they wouldn't get nipped on frosty nights. The maples and birches turned bright colors and the wind shook them and they dropped their leaves one by one to the ground. Under the wild apple trees in the pasture, the red little apples lay thick on the ground, and the sheep gnawed them and the geese gnawed them and foxes came in the night and sniffed them. One evening, just before Christmas, snow began falling. It covered house and barn and fields and woods. Wilbur had never seen snow before. When morning came he went out and plowed the drifts in his yard, for the fun of it. Fern and Avery arrived, dragging a sled. They coasted down the lane and out onto the frozen pond in the pasture.

"Coasting is the most fun there is," said Avery.

"The most fun there is," retorted Fern, "is when the Ferris wheel stops and Henry and I are in the top car and Henry makes the car swing and we can see everything for miles and miles and miles."

"Goodness, are you still thinking about that ol' Ferris wheel?" said Avery in disgust. "The Fair was weeks and weeks ago."

"I think about it all the time," said Fern, picking snow from her ear.

After Christmas the thermometer dropped to ten below zero. Cold settled on the world. The pasture was bleak and frozen. The cows stayed in the barn all the time now, except on sunny mornings when they went out and stood in the barnyard in the lee of the straw pile. The sheep stayed near the barn, too, for protection. When they were thirsty they ate snow. The geese hung around the barnyard the way boys hang around a drug store, and Mr. Zuckerman fed them corn and turnips to keep them cheerful.

"Many, many, many thanks!" they always said, when they saw food coming.

Templeton moved indoors when winter came. His ratty home under the pig trough was too chilly, so he fixed himself a cozy nest in the barn behind the grain bins. He lined it with bits of dirty newspapers and rags, and whenever he found a trinket or a keepsake he carried it home and stored it there. He continued to visit Wilbur three times a day, exactly at mealtime, and Wilbur kept the promise he had made. Wilbur let the rat eat first. Then, when Templeton couldn't hold another mouthful, Wilbur would eat. As a result of overeating, Templeton grew bigger and fatter than any rat you ever saw. He was gigantic. He was as big as a young woodchuck.

The old sheep spoke to him about his size one day. "You would live longer," said the old sheep, "if you ate less."

"Who wants to live forever?" sneered the rat. "I am naturally a heavy eater and I get untold satisfaction from the pleasures of the feast." He patted his stomach, grinned at the sheep, and crept upstairs to lie down.

All winter Wilbur watched over Charlotte's egg sac as though he were guarding his own children. He had scooped out a special place in the manure for the sac, next to the board fence. On very cold nights he lay so that his breath would warm it. For Wilbur, nothing in life was so important as this small round object—nothing else mattered. Patiently he awaited the end of winter and the coming of the little spiders. Life is always a rich and steady time when you are waiting for something to happen or to hatch. The winter ended at last.

"I heard the frogs today," said the old sheep one evening. "Listen! You can hear them now."

Wilbur stood still and cocked his ears. From the pond, in shrill chorus, came the voices of hundreds of little frogs.

"Springtime," said the old sheep, thoughtfully. "Another spring." As she walked away, Wilbur saw a new lamb following her. It was only a few hours old.

The snows melted and ran away. The streams and ditches bubbled and chattered with rushing water. A sparrow with a streaky breast arrived and sang. The light strengthened, the mornings came sooner. Almost every morning there was another new lamb in the sheepfold. The goose was sitting on nine eggs. The sky seemed wider and a warm wind blew. The last remaining strands of Charlotte's old web floated away and vanished.

One fine sunny morning, after breakfast, Wilbur

stood watching his precious sac. He wasn't thinking of anything much. As he stood there, he noticed something move. He stepped closer and stared. A tiny spider crawled from the sac. It was no bigger than a grain of sand, no bigger than the head of a pin. Its body was grey with a black stripe underneath. Its legs were grey and tan. It looked just like Charlotte.

Wilbur trembled all over when he saw it. The little spider waved at him. Then Wilbur looked more closely. Two more little spiders crawled out and waved. They climbed round and round on the sac, exploring their new world. Then three more little spiders. Then eight. Then ten. Charlotte's children were here at last.

Wilbur's heart pounded. He began to squeal. Then he raced in circles, kicking manure into the air. Then he turned a back flip. Then he planted his front feet and came to a stop in front of Charlotte's children.

"Hello, there!" he said.

The first spider said hello, but its voice was so small Wilbur couldn't hear it.

"I am an old friend of your mother's," said Wilbur. "I'm glad to see you. Are you all right? Is everything all right?"

The little spiders waved their forelegs at him. Wilbur could see by the way they acted that they were glad to see him.

"Is there anything I can get you? Is there anything you need?"

The young spiders just waved. For several days and several nights they crawled here and there, up and down, around and about, waving at Wilbur, trailing tiny draglines behind them, and exploring their home. There were dozens and dozens of them. Wilbur couldn't count them, but he knew that he had a great many new friends. They grew quite rapidly. Soon each was as big as a BB shot. They made tiny webs near the sac.

Then came a quiet morning when Mr. Zuckerman opened a door on the north side. A warm draft of rising air blew softly through the barn cellar. The air smelled of the damp earth, of the spruce woods, of the sweet springtime. The baby spiders felt the warm updraft. One spider climbed to the top of the fence. Then it did something that came as a great surprise to Wilbur. The spider stood on its head, pointed its spinnerets in the air, and let loose a cloud of fine silk. The silk formed a balloon. As Wilbur watched, the spider let go of the fence and rose into the air.

"Good-bye!" it said, as it sailed through the doorway.

"Wait a minute!" screamed Wilbur. "Where do you think you're going?"

But the spider was already out of sight. Then another

baby spider crawled to the top of the fence, stood on
its head, made a balloon, and sailed away. Then another
spider. Then another. The air was soon filled with tiny
balloons, each balloon carrying a spider.

Wilbur was frantic. Charlotte's babies were disap-
pearing at a great rate.

"Come back, children!" he cried.

"Good-bye!" they called. "Good-bye, good-bye!"

At last one little spider took time enough to stop and
talk to Wilbur before making its balloon.

"We're leaving here on the warm updraft. This is
our moment for setting forth. We are aeronauts and we

are going out into the world to make webs for ourselves."

"But *where?*" asked Wilbur.

"Wherever the wind takes us. High, low. Near, far.
East, west. North, south. We take to the breeze, we
go as we please."

"Are *all* of you going?" asked Wilbur. "You can't
all go. I would be left alone, with no friends. Your
mother wouldn't want that to happen, I'm sure."

The air was now so full of balloonists that the barn
cellar looked almost as though a mist had gathered.
Balloons by the dozen were rising, circling, and drift-
ing away through the door, sailing off on the gentle
wind. Cries of "Good-bye, good-bye, good-bye!" came
weakly to Wilbur's ears. He couldn't bear to watch
any more. In sorrow he sank to the ground and closed
his eyes. This seemed like the end of the world, to be
deserted by Charlotte's children. Wilbur cried himself
to sleep.

When he woke it was late afternoon. He looked at
the egg sac. It was empty. He looked into the air. The
balloonists were gone. Then he walked drearily to the
doorway, where Charlotte's web used to be. He was
standing there, thinking of her, when he heard a small
voice.

"Salutations!" it said. "I'm up here."

"So am I," said another tiny voice.

"So am I," said a third voice. "Three of us are staying. We like this place, and we like *you*."

Wilbur looked up. At the top of the doorway three small webs were being constructed. On each web, working busily was one of Charlotte's daughters.

"Can I take this to mean," asked Wilbur, "that you have definitely decided to live here in the barn cellar, and that I am going to have *three* friends?"

"You can indeed," said the spiders.

"What are your names, please?" asked Wilbur, trembling with joy.

"I'll tell you my name," replied the first little spider, "if you'll tell me why you are trembling."

"I'm trembling with joy," said Wilbur.

"Then my name is Joy," said the first spider.

"What was my mother's middle initial?" asked the second spider.

"A," said Wilbur.

"Then my name is Aranea," said the spider.

"How about me?" asked the third spider. "Will you just pick out a nice sensible name for me—something not too long, not too fancy, and not too dumb?"

Wilbur thought hard.

"Nellie?" he suggested.

"Fine, I like that very much," said the third spider. "You may call me Nellie." She daintily fastened her orb line to the next spoke of the web.

Wilbur's heart brimmed with happiness. He felt that he should make a short speech on this very important occasion.

"Joy! Aranea! Nellie!" he began. "Welcome to the barn cellar. You have chosen a hallowed doorway from which to string your webs. I think it is only fair to tell you that I was devoted to your mother. I owe my very life to her. She was brilliant, beautiful, and loyal to the end. I shall always treasure her memory. To you, her daughters, I pledge my friendship, forever and ever."

"I pledge mine," said Joy.

"I do, too," said Aranea.

"And so do I," said Nellie, who had just managed to catch a small gnat.

It was a happy day for Wilbur. And many more happy, tranquil days followed.

As time went on, and the months and years came and went, he was never without friends. Fern did not come regularly to the barn any more. She was growing up, and was careful to avoid childish things, like sitting on a milk stool near a pigpen. But Charlotte's children and grandchildren and great grandchildren, year after year, lived in the doorway. Each spring there were new little spiders hatching out to take the place of the old. Most of them sailed away, on their balloons. But always two or three stayed and set up housekeeping in the doorway.

Mr. Zuckerman took fine care of Wilbur all the rest of his days, and the pig was often visited by friends and admirers, for nobody ever forgot the year of his triumph and the miracle of the web. Life in the barn was very good—night and day, winter and summer, spring and fall, dull days and bright days. It was the best place to be, thought Wilbur, this warm delicious cellar, with the garrulous geese, the changing seasons, the heat of the sun, the passage of swallows, the nearness of rats, the sameness of sheep, the love of spiders, the smell of manure, and the glory of everything.

Wilbur never forgot Charlotte. Although he loved her children and grandchildren dearly, none of the new spiders ever quite took her place in his heart. She was in a class by herself. It is not often that someone comes along who is a true friend and a good writer. Charlotte was both.

THE END

TURN THE PAGE FOR THESE
SPECIAL FEATURES!

• A note to the reader from E. B. White •

• Letters from editor Ursula Nordstrom •

• Discussion questions •

A Note to the Reader from E. B. White

Dear Reader:

I receive many letters from children and can't answer them all—there wouldn't be time enough in a day. That is why I am sending you this printed reply to your letter. I'll try to answer some of the questions that are commonly asked.

Where did I get the idea for *Stuart Little* and for *Charlotte's Web*? Well, many years ago I went to bed one night in a railway sleeping car, and during the night I dreamed about a tiny boy who acted rather like a mouse. That's how the story of *Stuart Little* got started.

As for *Charlotte's Web*, I like animals and my barn is a very pleasant place to be, at all hours. One day when I was on my way to feed the pig, I began feeling sorry for the pig because, like most pigs, he was doomed to die. This made me sad. So I started thinking of ways to save a pig's life. I had been watching a big grey spider at her work and was impressed by how clever she was at weaving. Gradually I worked the spider into the story that you know, a story of friendship and salvation on a farm. Three years after I started writing it, it was published. (I am not a fast worker, as you can see.)

Sometimes I'm asked how old I was when I started to write, and what made me want to write. I started early—as soon as I could spell. In fact, I can't remember any time in my life when I wasn't busy writing. I don't know what caused me to do it, or why I enjoyed it, but I think children often find pleasure and satisfaction in trying to set their thoughts down on paper, either in words or in pictures. I was no good at drawing, so I used words instead. As I grew older, I found that writing can

3

be a way of earning a living.

Some of my readers want me to visit their school. Some want me to send a picture, or an autograph, or a book. And some ask questions about my family and my animals and my pets. Much as I'd like to, I can't go visiting. I can't send books, either—you can find them in a bookstore or a library. Many children assume that a writer owns (or even makes) his own books. This is not true—books are made by the publisher. If a writer wants a copy, he must buy it. That's why I can't send books. And I do not send autographs—I leave that to the movie stars. I live most of the year in the country, in New England. From our windows we can look out at the sea and the mountains. I live near my married son and three grandchildren.

Are my stories true, you ask? No, they are imaginary tales, containing fantastic characters and events. In real life, a family doesn't have a child who looks like a mouse; in real life, a spider doesn't spin words in her web. In real life, a swan doesn't blow a trumpet. But real life is only one kind of life—there is also the life of the imagination. And although my stories are imaginary, I like to think that there is some truth in them, too—truth about the way people and animals feel and think and act.

Yours sincerely,

E. B. White

Ursula Nordstrom was the director of Harper's Department of Books for Boys and Girls from 1940 through 1973. With her dry wit, blunt honesty, and focus on appealing directly to young readers, Nordstrom was hugely influential in creating children's literature as we know it today. During her time at HarperCollins, she published classic children's books by such iconic authors as Margaret Wise Brown, Shel Silverstein, Maurice Sendak, John Steptoe, and of course, E. B. White.

TO E. B. WHITE
March 19, 1951
Dear Mr. White:

Thanks for your letter telling me you've recently finished another children's book. That's the best news I've had in a long long time.

We assume that you will want Garth Williams to illustrate it and I'm warning him to keep his schedule as flexible as possible. We know you can't possibly say when you think "the body heat" will go out of your story, and we'll welcome it whenever it comes. I'll just keep hoping that Garth won't be in the middle of anything with an urgent deadline for Simon & Schuster. Any Harper book he ever does is given to him with the understanding that he can stop work on it the minute the E. B. White manuscript arrives. I wish I could speak as firmly for S & S!

I've been a little afraid to answer your letter. I don't want to write anything that might seem pushy. I hope I haven't.

Yours sincerely,

[signature]

TO E. B. WHITE

April 2, 1952

Dear Andy:

I am glad you are too exhausted to call me Miss Nordstrom any longer. We will save a great deal of typing time.

The copy of *American Spiders* came and we sent it right down to Garth. We also sent him the New York Public Library slip on the McCook books. As you have probably heard from him, he loves *Charlotte's Web* as much as I do and is at work on the illustrations. You'll see some soon.

The Advertising Department is preparing copy for *Charlotte's Web* and we will send it to you for your comments. There is no rush for jacket copy, of course, but there is for catalogue copy.

No, I have never encountered any story plot like *Charlotte's Web*. I do not believe that any other writer has ever told about a spider writing words in its web. Perhaps I should ask some of the children's book ladies who go back even further in time than I do, but I am sure nothing even remotely like this has been written. I believe Charlotte is the first spider since Miss Muffet's.

Yours sincerely,

Ursula Nordstrom

TO E. B. WHITE

October 23, 1952

Dear Andy:

Thanks for your letter. I enclose a review which will appear in the next issue of *The Horn Book*.

And thanks for the grave comment of Caroline Angell. I am

absolutely sure that most children will love the book, even more than *Stuart Little*. The children I know love it, including one tough nine-year-old boy who states it is his favorite book. Please don't worry at all about the children.

Rumors have reached me that Miss Anne Carroll Moore has certain reservations about *Charlotte's Web*. As her reservations about *Stuart Little* preceded a wonderful success for that book I am taking all this as good news for *Charlotte's Web*. (I would not mention this but someone may quote Miss Moore to you.) Well, Eudora Welty said the book was perfect for anyone over eight or under eighty, and that leaves Miss Moore out as she is a girl of eighty-two.

I will stop writing you so many letters soon.

Yours,

[signature]

TO —— *a school child*
February 16, 1973
Dear——:
Your letter about Charlotte's death has come to me because I published the book, *Charlotte's Web*. When I read the manuscript I felt exactly the way you now feel. I didn't want Charlotte to die, and I too cried over her death.

What I think you and I both should keep in mind is that Charlotte had a good and worthwhile life. And she was a true friend to Wilbur. And something to be glad about is that she had all those children. I think the author knows that in due course a spider such as Charlotte does die, but her children live, and so will her children's children.

This may not be of much comfort to you now, but perhaps as time goes by you will understand why E. B. White had to tell Charlotte's story the way he told it.

Thank you very much for writing, and for sharing your feelings with us.

Yours sincerely,

Discussion Questions

The following questions align with the Common Core State Standards for Reading Literature and Speaking and Listening as follows: RL.4.1, RL.4.2, RL.4.3, RL.4.4, RL.4.10, RL.4.11; SL.4.1, SL.4.3, SL.4.4.

1. In chapter 1, Fern is very upset that her father is going to destroy Wilbur because he is a runt. She argues until he agrees to spare the pig. Her father says that Fern is "trying to rid the world of injustice." What does he mean by this?

2. How does Fern show her parents that she is responsible enough to care for Wilbur?

3. In chapter 3, Wilbur escapes from his pen. How does he feel when he frees himself? How do Wilbur's feelings change as the chapter progresses?

4. *Charlotte's Web* takes place on Mr. Zuckerman's farm. Describe the setting of this story. What animals live on the farm? What does the farm look like?

5. In chapter 5, Wilbur reflects upon his new friendship with Charlotte. He is happy to have a new friend, but he is worried about some of her qualities. He says, "I've got a new friend, all right. But what a gamble friendship is!" What worries Wilbur about Charlotte? Which of her traits does he admire?

6. In chapter 5, Charlotte explains that she must "live by my wits." What does she mean by this? Think of examples of people living by their wits. In what ways do you live by your wits?

7. In chapter 9, Charlotte compares her life to the lives of others. She says people "rush, rush, rush, every minute . . . I stay put and wait for what comes. Gives me a chance to think." Think about your own lifestyle. Do you rush from one activity to the next, or do you have time at home to relax and think? Which do you enjoy more, going from place to place or spending time relaxing and thinking? Which do you think is more important? Why?

8. Fern and her brother, Avery, spend their days on the farm swinging on a rope swing, building a tree house, catching frogs, and picking raspberries. Do you think these activities are similar or different from what a lot of kids do for fun today? What activities do you like to do?

9. Charlotte is desperate to save her friend Wilbur's life, and she's determined to come up with a plan. What are the disadvantages Charlotte faces as a spider trying to save a pig's life? When Charlotte was planning, were you able to predict what she would do? If you were in Charlotte's place, what would your plan have been? Do you think it would have worked?

10. When Charlotte put her plan into action (chapter 11), how does Mr. Zuckerman react?

11. Mr. Zuckerman tells his wife, "Our pig is completely out of the ordinary" (chapter 11). What other characters in this story are extraordinary? Why?

12. When Charlotte's plan starts to work, Wilbur becomes a famous pig. Fern is happy that Wilbur will be saved, but finds that things on the farm have changed. In what way do things change? How does Fern feel about these changes?

13. In chapter 12, Charlotte says, "People believe almost anything they see in print." Do you think that's true? How does that statement relate to Charlotte's plan?

14. In chapter 13, Charlotte decides to weave "TERRIFIC" into her web. What does she do to help herself complete this difficult task? What facts do you learn about spiders in this chapter?

15. At first Wilbur is embarrassed that Charlotte is going to write "TERRIFIC" in her web, but eventually he begins to feel that he really is terrific. Why do you think Wilbur's feelings about himself change?

16. In chapter 14, Fern says that her "best friends are in the barn cellar," but by chapter 20, Fern is excited about spending time with her friend Henry Fussy.

How has Fern changed from the beginning of the book to the end?

17. Read chapter 15. How has fame affected Wilbur? What is the most important thing in his life?

18. In chapter 16, after the old sheep tells Templeton about the food at the Fair Grounds, why does Charlotte wink at the sheep?

19. In chapter 18, when Wilbur asks Charlotte if she thinks that Mr. Zuckerman will let him live, how does Charlotte reassure him?

20. In chapter 19, Charlotte describes the egg sac she has created. How does the sac protect the eggs inside?

21. In chapter 19, Charlotte writes "humble" in her web. What does humble mean? Is this an appropriate word to describe Wilbur? How does Wilbur respond when he wins the prize at the fair?

22. In chapter 21, Wilbur recalls how he first felt about Charlotte. How have his feelings about Charlotte changed?

23. Charlotte saves Wilbur's future, and Wilbur saves Charlotte's future. How does each character accomplish this?

More great Harper Classics!

Katherine Paterson

E. B. White
PICTURES BY GARTH WILLIAMS

Neil Gaiman
WITH ILLUSTRATIONS BY DAVE McKEAN

Thanhhà Lại

C. S. Lewis

Beverly Cleary

Katherine Applegate

Sharon Creech